LEOPA

Elizabeth Laird was b̲ when she was three the̲ ̲ ̲ ̲ ̲ ̲ ̲ to England. Since then she has travel̲ ̲ ̲ ̲ to the furthest corners of the world and has encountered all kinds of animals. On one adventure she became lost at night in a Kenyan game reserve, coming a little too close to an angry rhino and narrowly avoiding buffalo and elephants. Her experience of the wild animals of Africa has helped her write the *Wild Things* series.

She is the award-winning author of *Red Sky in the Morning*, *Kiss the Dust*, *Secret Friends* (shortlisted for the 1997 Carnegie Medal) and many other children's novels.

Elizabeth Laird has been helped in her research for *Wild Things* by wildlife experts and local people in Kenya, whose lives are constantly touched by the animals amongst which they live.

All Wild Things titles can be ordered at your local bookshop or are available by post from Book Service by Post (tel: 01624 675137).

WILD THINGS

LEOPARD TRAIL

Elizabeth Laird

MACMILLAN CHILDREN'S BOOKS

Series consultant: Dr Shirley Strum
with the support of Dr David Western,
past director of the Kenya Wildlife Service

First published 1999 by Macmillan Children's Books
a division of Macmillan Publishers Limited
25 Eccleston Place, London SW1W 9NF
Basingstoke and Oxford
www.macmillan.co.uk

Associated companies throughout the world

ISBN 0 330 37148 7

5 7 9 8 6

A CIP catalogue record for this book is available from
the British Library.

Phototypeset by Intype London Ltd
Printed and bound in Great Britain by
Mackays of Chatham plc, Kent

For Scilla and Rob

because from their house in Nairobi (where they looked after me so kindly) I watched the rain sweep over the Ngong hills, and heard monkeys on the roof, and wondered about the mysterious strip of forest just beyond the garden fence.

Something stirred in the long yellow grass. A herd of impala skittered, ready for flight. A buffalo lifted his black horned head and his darting eyes scanned the landscape. A zebra flicked his tail over his tight-striped rump and stamped a shiny black hoof on the baked red earth.

The hawk, floating on the warm air above the sweeping plain, was the only one to see the sinuous creature, creeping on its velvet belly through the brittle stalks. She saw round ears pricked to catch the slightest sound, nostrils flared to sniff at the warm breeze, and two golden eyes, under a heavy brow, searching the way ahead.

The leopard was hunting.

It was days since he had had a decent meal. He had been with his mother until a month ago, sharing her kills and learning the leopard's craft from her. But he was grown up now and knew all that she could teach him. For some time they had been sparring, baring their teeth and snarling at each other. Then she had driven him away, off her territory, sending him out into the world to find a place of his own.

He had hunted every night, as she had taught him, without much success. Now he was driven to the harder task of hunting during the day.

The young leopard stiffened. He had caught the scent of a gazelle. He crouched, ready to spring. The gazelle, sensing something wrong, raised her head and sniffed the air. The leopard crawled forward, every muscle taut. He sprang. But the gazelle was too quick for him. She dodged aside, then fled for her life on flashing hooves, zigzagging away from his outstretched claws.

He chased her for a while, then gave up, exhausted. He would never catch her now.

The harsh African sun beat down on the open plain. The leopard made for a tree that stood, a single sentinel, above the dry grass. Wearily, he climbed it and stretched out on a branch to watch and wait. Then he fell asleep.

When he woke it was late in the afternoon. He lifted his head and looked out across the plain towards the strange thing in the distance, the mass of tall blocks and shiny surfaces on which the sun glinted and from which came a rumble of noise made by no animal that he knew of.

The distant city frightened him but interested him too. He could see a wooded valley running towards it. Woodland might be a good place to hide and hunt. Perhaps he would have more luck there.

He yawned, stretched himself, then leapt lightly down from the tree and loped off towards the suburbs of Nairobi.

1

WAKING UP IN AFRICA

Scrabbling noises on the roof half woke Tom. He turned over, and his knuckles grazed the wall beside his bed. He frowned without opening his eyes. Something was wrong. The wall should be on the other side of the bed. Vaguely, he realized that the noises in his room were wrong too. There was no traffic from the road outside. Instead there were strange bird calls and that funny scratching noise on the roof.

Suddenly, Tom woke up properly and sat bolt upright in bed.

Africa! He was in Africa! He'd slept his first night in the new house in Nairobi!

He looked round the bare-walled bedroom. They'd arrived after dark last night and all he'd seen of Africa so far was a confused jumble of trees and streets and wayside houses picked out in the lights of the taxi. He'd been so tired when they'd arrived he'd walked in through the front door and fallen dead asleep on the sofa. Dad must have picked him up and carted him off to bed . . .

There it was again. That noise on the roof.

Tom jumped out of bed, pulled back the curtains and opened the window.

The light nearly dazzled him. The sun was just coming up. It lit up a distant range of purply blue hills and the green sweep of land in between, and it sparkled on the big glossy leaves of the tall tree just outside his window and the spikes of a palm halfway down the garden.

It was their garden now, he supposed. He didn't want to like it, because it didn't have the old shed and the swing and the broken front gate of his old garden back home in England. But he couldn't help feeling a little stirring of excitement. This garden was huge. There was a stretch of grass, too patchy to be called a lawn, with shrubs and trees dotted about on it, and more bushes running along the fence. Beyond the fence was what looked like a sort of woodland, with thick trees and undergrowth.

A bird, the biggest Tom had ever seen in the wild (except for the swans and Canada geese in the park at home) suddenly flew right across the garden, landed in the palm tree and began to sing in bell-like, running notes.

There was a burst of noise from the roof right over Tom's window and a small furry body launched itself into the tree, too fast for Tom to see clearly. The branch swayed furiously and Tom saw a long black tail dangling down out of the leaves and, minutes later, a black head with deep-set dark eyes that had turned to stare at him.

A monkey! breathed Tom.

He dashed for his bedroom door.

'Mum! Dad!' he shouted. 'There's monkeys in the garden!'

The upstairs landing was quiet and empty and all the doors were closed. One of them must go into his parents' bedroom, and the other must be Bella's. He hesitated. He certainly didn't want to wake Bella. She'd whinge and whine and try to follow him everywhere. On second thoughts, he didn't want to wake his parents either. He'd rather explore on his own.

He ran down the stairs. Opposite him was the front door. He tried it. It was locked. On the right, the door into the sitting room was open. The sofa on which he'd fallen asleep last night was in the middle of the room, and there were piles and piles of huge cardboard boxes. A black cat with a white patch under his chin was lying asleep on one of them.

'Hey, Tiger,' said Tom. 'Are you OK?'

He picked the cat up. He'd been worried about her getting here safely, worried about her being OK with the man from Dad's company who'd collected her from the animal transit place. Seeing her framed in the doorway was the only thing he remembered about his arrival at the house last night.

'Good old Tiger,' said Tom. 'You're guarding all our stuff, aren't you?' He looked over the packing cases. 'My computer's somewhere in all this lot, I suppose. It had better be, anyway.'

Thinking of his computer made him think of his bedroom at home and he began to feel angry again. He'd been angry ever since Dad had told him they'd be moving to Africa. He'd hated leaving home and his old school and all his friends. He'd even thought of running away, and he and his best mate, Scott, had planned how he'd hide out in the old shed by the garages of the flats where Scott lived. They'd both known it was silly, but it had been kind of comforting, all the same.

Then he remembered the monkey.

Scott wouldn't believe this, he thought.

With Tiger in his arms, he ran to the French windows at the far end of the room, unlocked them and stepped out onto a verandah. It was quite big. There was a kind of vine growing over it on beams that made a leafy roof, and some basketwork armchairs and sofas. Two steps led down onto the grass.

It was cool, but there was a hint of warmth for the day to come. Tom took a deep breath. The air was tinglingly fresh and clean. Tom went down the top step and stood on the bottom one, looking at the grass. It wasn't like the grass at home. The blades were wider and coarser, and the earth in between them was a rich red colour.

Tom squinted up into the trees, narrowing his eyes against the light. Where was the monkey? He could hardly believe he'd seen it. The idea of a monkey in the garden was so amazing that anything seemed possible. Perhaps there was a zebra hiding behind the bushes, or a giraffe just round the corner by the garage, or a python coiled round a branch of one of those trees down there.

He stood still for a moment, feeling like an early explorer or the first man to set foot on the moon. Then he set off across the grass towards the row of shrubs and trees near the fence at the bottom of the garden.

He'd never seen plants like these before. There was one with big long leaves as tall as he was, and bushes of every imaginable shade of green. Some leaves weren't even green at all, but a deep crimson colour. They looked strange, shooting out of the russet-coloured earth.

Red's the colour of Africa, thought Tom.

He thought it might be fun to make a base somewhere in the bushes, and he was about to bend down and take a closer look when he heard something rustle in the dry leaves and he started back, afraid there might be a snake.

He looked up. There was no sign of the monkey. Nothing was moving in the trees.

Tom was under the palm now. Its trunk was rough and knobbly, like the skin of an enormous woody pineapple. He'd liked climbing trees at home, but he wouldn't bother with this one. He'd cut himself to bits.

There were a couple more quite tall trees in the other corner of the garden. Tom went over to look at them, peering up between the branches in case the monkey was still hiding up there, but no black wizened face looked down at him. The trunks of these trees were smoother than the palm, dappled with pale green lichens and patches of moss, and the leaves overhead were fleshy and glossier than the trees at home. He put his hand on one of the lower branches. He'd have a go at climbing it when he'd got out of his pyjamas and into some proper clothes.

Behind the trees, there was a high chain link fence which ran all the way round the perimeter of the garden. It seemed taller than a normal fence. Too tall, really, for an ordinary garden, as though it was there not so much to mark the garden's boundary as to keep things in. Or out.

Tom walked along it, peering through the mesh to see what was on the other side. He couldn't see much, though there was one place, on the right side of the garden, where he could just make out the shape of a long low building, half covered in creepers. At the bottom of the garden, low-growing trees and dense bushes grew right up against the boundary and it was impossible to make out anything more than a couple of metres away.

Suddenly he stopped. There was a place here where two sections of chain link met but hadn't been fixed together properly. If he pushed at one of them it sagged a bit and made a gap which he could squeeze through.

He was pushing at the fence, seeing how big the opening could be made, when he heard, in the still, clear air, a window opening in the house behind him. He looked back. His mother was leaning out of her bedroom window.

'Tom!' she called down to him. 'What are you doing out there? Get back inside quick!'

The window clicked shut. Reluctantly, Tom turned back towards the house. Halfway across the grass he thought of something and looked back towards the fence. The gap couldn't be seen from here. It was only visible if you were standing right beside it. He was pleased about that. He'd keep it for his own secret.

Debbie Wilkinson had come downstairs by the time he'd got back to the house and was waiting for him at the door that led from the sitting room to the verandah. She was wearing a pink towelling bathrobe, and her blond hair straggled down over her collar. She looked somehow softer at this time of day, before she'd put her make-up on. Tiger jumped off her perch on the packing case and began to rub herself against Debbie's feet.

'There's a monkey in the garden,' said Tom. 'I wanted to go and look for it.'

'I don't want you messing about out there!' Debbie's voice was sharp with anxiety. 'There might be snakes and spiders and goodness knows what else. Anyway, monkeys can give you rabies.'

'But it's our garden!' said Tom, in the complaining voice he always seemed forced to use with his mum. 'You've got to let me go out into my own garden!'

'Not till your dad's had a good look round first,' said Debbie.

She looked up at the vine that roofed the verandah.

'This verandah might be all right, I suppose,' she said doubtfully, 'though I'm a bit worried about all that greenery. Anything might drop down onto your head.'

Tom squinted up at the vine, half expecting to see the coils of a snake or a big black poisonous spider dangling from a length of silk, but all he could see was a mass of leaves and twisting stems.

'I'm not staying inside all day, anyway,' he said defiantly.

But Debbie wasn't listening to him any more. She'd heard a wail from upstairs and was already clacking across the wooden floor in her high-heeled mules.

'Bella! Poor little soul. She'll have woken up and not known where she is. Now you stay in here, Tom. You can make yourself useful and start opening the boxes. It'll take us days to unpack and get everything straight.'

2
BELLA

Tom explored the house. It was big, much bigger than the end-of-terrace house he'd always lived in back in England. Apart from the sitting room, which went right through to the back of the house and opened on to the verandah, there was a small room, which Mum said was going to be a kind of study for Dad, and a little room next to the kitchen, with a dining table and chairs in it, and the kitchen itself, with all the usual things, like a sink and a cooker and a fridge. He had to admit, it was a brilliant house.

Maybe it won't be so bad here after all, he thought. Maybe Mum and Dad'll get on a bit better, anyway.

Breakfast was a funny kind of meal. Someone from Dad's company had left the fridge full of food for them, so they had a weird kind of fruit, which Mum wouldn't touch but Dad said was absolutely delicious, and some bread rolls and mango jam. Bella whined for her favourite cereal, and Tom minded not having his, and Dad was being falsely cheerful, trying to persuade them all that coming to Nairobi had been a brilliant idea.

'I told you,' he kept saying. 'They're a good company, Murchisons. Got an eye for detail. I mean, everything's set up for us here. They've even stocked up the fridge. Best import-export company in East Africa. Known for it everywhere.'

'Thank you, Simon,' said Debbie drily. 'I know all about import-export. I had a great job, remember, in Customs and Excise, before you dragged me away from it and dumped me down here.'

'No, but look at this house!' Simon Wilkinson waved an enthusiastic hand. 'Right on the edge of Nairobi National Park! There's the most amazing wildlife there, and no more than a stone's throw from this house. Rhinos, zebras, wildebeest, cheetahs, baboons – you name it, they've got it. We'll have giraffes sticking their heads in through the bedroom windows, and lions gambolling on the lawn.'

No one said anything. Simon gave up the attempt, picked up Murchisons' last annual report and began reading it for the third time.

Only Tiger seemed quite happy. She'd jumped up into Tom's lap, which she wasn't supposed to do at mealtimes, and Tom had pulled his chair further in under the table, so that Debbie wouldn't notice, and had kept her there all through breakfast, not stroking her in case she purred and gave herself away.

The window was in front of Tom. He could look out into the bushes outside, and all the time, Africa and its purple hills and the garden and the palm tree and the gap in the hedge were waiting, while he was stuck in here, bursting to get out.

After breakfast, Dad got the first box open.

'What have we got in here then?' he said breezily, folding back the stiff cardboard flaps and picking up a tattered green stuffed crocodile. 'Look, Tom, it's Crocker! What did you bring him out here for? I thought you'd grown out of cuddly toys.'

'I have,' said Tom, snatching the crocodile out of his father's hands. 'Mum must have packed it.'

Embarrassed, he dropped Crocker over the back of the sofa, out of his father's sight.

Simon Wilkinson was pulling out a couple of board game boxes.

'I think it's all your stuff in here,' he said. 'I'll get it up to your room and you can unpack it yourself.'

He picked the box up and went out through the sitting-room door into the hall. Tom heard him say, 'Mind out, sweetheart. Daddy will trip over you if you lie right there,' then his father's footsteps went on up the stairs.

Tom was opening the Monopoly game on the top of the pile that Dad had put down on the table to check if all the pieces were still in it when he became aware of someone breathing heavily through a snuffly nose beside him, and he looked round to see Bella, standing by the sofa, holding Crocker in her arms. She was staring at him expectantly, her big blue eyes wide open.

'Put Crocker down,' said Tom.

Bella squeezed Crocker against her chest and waited.

'There's monkeys in the garden,' said Tom, knowing from experience that the direct approach seldom worked with Bella. 'Go and look out of the window.'

He'd hoped to excite Bella enough to make her drop Crocker, but it didn't work. Bella's grip on the crocodile tightened.

'I saw one with a long tail,' said Tom.

'Want Crocker,' said Bella. 'Don't like monkeys.'

Tom lost patience, jumped over the low coffee table in front of the sofa and snatched Crocker out of Bella's arms. She was taken by surprise, sat down suddenly and knocked her head lightly on the corner of the coffee table. Tom watched in disgust, knowing what would happen next. Bella's face went red and her mouth opened. For a long moment nothing came out of it, then she gave a shuddering scream that made Tom clap his hands over his ears.

Debbie came running into the room.

'Tom! What have you done now?' she said accusingly.

'What do you mean?' Tom's face was red now. 'That's so unfair! It's always me. Why don't you ever . . .'

Debbie had scooped Bella up in her arms. The screams had turned to bellows.

'Crocker!' Bella was yelling. 'I want Crocker!'

Too late, Tom hid Crocker behind his back. Debbie had seen it.

'Crocker?' said Debbie crossly. 'Is that what all the fuss is about? Give it to Bella, Tom.'

Tom's fist tightened round the crocodile's tail.

'No!' he said. 'Why should I? She takes all my stuff, wrecks everything, she's not having . . .'

A deafening wail from Bella interrupted him. Debbie cradled her against her neck.

'Never mind, darling,' she crooned. 'Mummy'll get you a drink.' Her cheek had been lying against Bella's straight mouse-coloured hair, but now she lifted her head and glared at Tom. 'She's only three,' she said, 'and all this is very unsettling for her. I do think you might show a bit more consideration for . . .'

'What about me?' shouted Tom. 'Why is she the only one who's supposed to be unsettled? Who's showing consideration for me?'

Simon Wilkinson appeared in the doorway.

'Don't you shout at your mother like that,' he said. 'You can go up to your room and stay there. Do something useful. Sort out your stuff.'

Tom pushed past him, bounded up the stairs

and wrenched open his bedroom door. Tiger, lying on his bed, looked up at him. Tom shoved Crocker as far under his bed as he could reach and flung himself down beside Tiger.

'You're the only person I like in this family,' he said, 'and you're not even a human being.'

3

THE DIKDIK BY THE POOL

Tiger jumped off Tom's bed, stalked over to the packing case, which Simon had dumped down on the floor of Tom's room, and sniffed at it. Then she sprang lightly up onto it and began to claw at the cardboard flaps that covered it.

Tom got up and began pulling things out of the packing case. His stuff looked strange here. It was nice to see it all again, to feel that he'd still got it and that it had arrived OK, but nothing seemed quite the same. His huge motorbike poster had looked great above his bed at home, but there wasn't an obvious place for it in this room. There was no table for his computer, either, and nowhere to put his stack of games.

The room was a mess now and he didn't feel like tidying up. He looked round, wondering where he could put everything.

There was a high round window in the wall opposite the door that he hadn't really noticed before. He went over to it and looked out.

He could just see the house next door. It was a bungalow. The roof was made of strips of corrugated iron, old and dull and rusty, and one corner of it was buried under brilliant orange flowers. There was a big garden round the house, quite overgrown, with a small patch of lawn and a lot of tall trees and clumps of bushes.

As he watched, an African woman in a bright yellow dress came out of the house, carrying a dish in her hand.

'Mama! Give it to me!' someone called out, and a boy, who looked about the same age as Tom, came out after her.

That was when Tom heard the noise on the roof again. The monkey! He jumped off the bed and ran over to the big window that looked down towards the bottom of the garden. He opened the window and leaned out as far as he dared. He couldn't see anything.

I've got to get outside, he thought. I've got to see it.

He opened his bedroom door. No one was around. He could hear Dad and Mum moving about downstairs and the jingly sound of cartoon music coming from the sitting room. They must have put a video on for Bella.

He crept down the stairs. The front door was ajar. It was going to be easy, after all. He slipped through it and was out of the house.

He turned left and ran round the side of the house, ducking down under the kitchen window in case anyone inside saw him. When he came to the corner where his bedroom was, he looked up.

It's gone, he thought.

Disappointed, he kicked at the grass.

Then, from the tree behind him, he heard a rustling of leaves. He turned round. The monkey was sitting on a branch, looking at him, its head tilted enquiringly to one side. One elegant black hand was holding on to the branch and the other was raised, almost as if it was waving to him. The monkey looked so curious and intelligent, so altogether human, that Tom nearly burst out laughing.

Tom smiled and held out his hand.

'Come here,' he said softly. 'I won't hurt you.'

He took a step towards the tree. The monkey bared its teeth and chattered angrily. It ran down the branch towards the end, then took a flying leap, its tail streaming out behind, towards the big tree on the far side of the garden fence. It landed with a crash of violently shaken leaves and seconds later had disappeared, leaving the branch behind it bouncing up and down as it regained its equilibrium.

Tom let out his breath. He'd seen monkeys before, on TV lots of times and once in a zoo, but he'd never imagined they could be like this – so energetic, so alive and wild and free. He wanted to feel free, too. He wanted to get out of the garden, to explore the forest beyond.

He ran quickly down towards the gap in the fence, looking over his shoulder a couple of times to make sure no one was watching him from the house.

It was harder squeezing through the gap than he'd thought it would be. The jagged ends of wire caught at his T-shirt and he had to stop and work it free.

Once on the other side, he hesitated, looking ahead into the dense undergrowth. It might be silly to go on alone. At home, in a place like this, he'd be afraid of thieves or junkies or sex maniacs but here there were other things to fear – snakes, huge sinister insects, big animals like lions or leopards even. If something did happen to him, no one would know where he was. They wouldn't even know where to start looking for him.

Then he saw that there was a kind of tunnel with low overhanging branches running through the undergrowth. It would be easy to follow if he ducked right down. He lowered his head and started out along it. It wasn't too bad after the first few metres. The track widened out and the bushes separated so that he could stand up.

He was going downhill all the time.

I must remember this, he thought, for when I come back.

He tried to notice things, an oddly shaped branch or a tuft of fluffy grey green leaves, that could act as signposts.

The track turned a sudden corner and he came out on to a wider one, a proper path. He looked for a marker to show him where to find his turn-off again. It would be easy. There was a cluster of big red-hot poker flowers shooting out of a clump of spiky leaves.

Tom ran on. Once or twice, he heard a strange sound, a rustling in the leaves, or the warning cries of unfamiliar birds, but each time, when he stopped, the noises stopped too and encouraged, he went on, slipping occasionally on the stones that rose up, round and smooth, out of the hard earth.

He sensed that he was nearly at the bottom. He heard a rustle overhead and looked up, hoping to see the monkey again, missed his footing and fell forwards, grabbing hold of the nearest plant. It was a trailing vine covered with sharp thorns and they bit deeply into the palm of his hand. He grunted with the sudden pain, but went on.

He reached the bottom of the hill and came out into a kind of forest glade. A stream ran past along the valley floor, spilling gently from one clear pool to the next. A little antelope was drinking at one of them. It was tiny, no bigger than a hare, and for a moment Tom thought it was a perfect miniature statue. Then he gasped in amazement as it lifted its head and saw him. For a second Tom could see the sunlight glowing pinkly through its delicate pricked ears and the shiny black hooves that tipped its fragile legs, one of which was raised as it prepared to bolt. Then with a leap it was away, off into the bushes on the far side of the stream, and Tom caught no more than a final glimpse of its round little rump as it disappeared.

'OK, dumbo. Thanks a million. Thanks a whole big heap.'

Tom spun round. A girl was crouching on a rock beside the stream, one long thin brown arm still stretched out towards the pool where the little antelope had been drinking. Her dark eyes scowled at him from under a tangle of frizzy black hair and her voice crackled with hostility.

Tom stared back at her over the lacerated hand he was sucking.

'What's the matter with you?' he said. 'What am I supposed to have done?'

'What did you do? You only scared off the dikdik that I nearly had eating out of my hand after weeks and weeks of trying. That's all,' the girl said.

'How was I supposed to know? I've never been here before,' said Tom, offended.

The girl looked at him for a long moment, then she shook the hair away from her oval, pale-brown face as if she was shaking away her irritation, and sighed.

'What are you doing here anyway? No one ever comes here, except me and Joseph.'

'I live here,' said Tom. 'Up there.'

He jerked his thumb in the direction of his house.

'Oh!' the girl nodded. 'You're the new people next door. The two-year wonders.'

'What do you mean?' said Tom.

'You come here for a couple of years, think you own the place, and then go home again. Like the people who were in your house before.'

'I don't even know them,' said Tom. 'I never even met them. We only came yesterday.'

'So you didn't know Susie? She was supposed to be my friend. But she went off back to England and never even said goodbye.'

'Well, that's hardly my fault, is it?' said Tom. 'And if you think . . .'

He let out a sudden yelp of terror and started back. Something was touching his leg. An animal was pressed up against him. He looked down. It was Tiger.

The girl had burst out laughing.

'Scared of a pussy cat, are you?' she said. 'You'll never get along out here. This is Africa, dumbo.'

She watched as Tom bent down, picked Tiger up and held her protectively in his arms.

'That your cat?'

'Yes. She's called Tiger.'

'Tiger's a male name.'

'So?'

The girl's eyes were still on the cat.

'She's nice.' She made a mewing noise and squatted down. To Tom's annoyance, Tiger wriggled out of his arms, ran across to the girl and began to rub her back against the girl's bare brown leg. The girl picked her up and expertly stroked the little cat's favourite place under her chin.

'My name's Afra. Afra Elizabeth Tovey,' the girl said, looking up at Tom.

'I'm Tom,' said Tom unwillingly. 'Tom Wilkinson.'

'You'd better watch out for Tiger,' said Afra, and Tom heard a softer note in her voice. 'There's a leopard about. A cat's no more than a chocolate bar to a leopard.'

'A leopard?' said Tom. 'What? Here? I don't believe you.'

'You'd better believe me. I'm telling you, it's true.'

In spite of himself, Tom looked uneasily over his shoulder.

'What are you doing here on your own then, if there's a leopard around?'

'It's a young one,' said Afra casually. 'It wouldn't go for me. It's not big enough.'

'How do you know?'

'I've seen its pug marks.'

'Its what?'

She cast her eyes up scornfully.

'Its footprints. In the mud.'

'Well then,' said Tom triumphantly, 'if you haven't actually seen it, you can't be sure it's really a leopard, can you? It might be a big dog, or a . . .'

'Give me a break,' said Afra, and stood up suddenly. She was tall, nearly as tall as Tom, and her long legs were encased in old blue cotton trousers. 'You have a sister, don't you?'

'How did you know that?'

Afra suddenly gave him a warm, dazzling smile. Dimples appeared in her pale brown cheeks and she chuckled.

'Everyone knows everything about everybody here,' she said. 'You'll get used to it. Your landlady told Prof.'

'Who's Prof?'

'My dad. He's a professor. I always call him Prof. Is it true? Do you have a sister?'

'Yes,' said Tom, 'but she's only three and she's a pain.'

'Oh.' Afra looked disappointed. Her smile faded and a serious expression came into her eyes. 'You'd better watch out for her,' she said. 'I mean it. A three-year-old kid – she'd just be a hamburger and fries to a leopard.'

Tom reached out and Afra reluctantly passed Tiger back to him. The cat mewed a protest, then took up her favourite position, lying over Tom's shoulder. He dropped his cheek down against her warm soft fur and she began to purr enthusiastically.

'Do you really mean it about the leopard?' said Tom.

Afra nodded.

'Sure I do.' She lifted her head and listened, as if she could hear someone calling her. 'I've got to go now. See you around.'

'Yeah,' said Tom. 'See you.'

He watched her run up the steep path, then, holding tightly to Tiger and looking nervously around him, he started up the hill himself, towards the track that led to the gap in the fence and home.

4

THE CHONGALULU

'You've got to be joking, Mum,' said Tom, looking at himself with horror in the mirror on his bedroom wall. No one goes to school in shorts. Not since the nineteenth century.'

Debbie looked at him doubtfully.

'It's what they said in the letter,' she said. 'Grey shorts, green shortsleeved shirt, green socks, brown shoes.'

'But I look a total freak,' said Tom.

'I can't have got it wrong,' said Debbie, not contradicting him. 'And the man at the shop on Saturday said it was right for St Peter's too.'

'Tom!' Simon Wilkinson called up the stairs. 'What are you doing? Get a move on. We're going to be late.'

Debbie put her arm round Tom's shoulders.

'It'll be all right, love,' she said. 'It's a lovely school, I'm sure. And there are a couple of other kids with dads at Murchisons. I'm sure you'll make friends with them.'

Tom shook her off and picked up his old school bag. It was purple and had two holograms as well as an Aston Villa badge sewn on to it. At least there was nothing weird about his bag.

'Tom!' yelled Simon again. 'Have I got to come up there and drag you downstairs?'

It was a long drive to the school. Tom had been out in the car a couple of times since he'd arrived in Nairobi two days ago, and he'd looked round curiously, trying to take in the new sights: the battered blue minibuses crammed with people, the roadside stalls selling everything from beds to bananas, the tall glass and steel offices in the centre of town, the brightly coloured clothes of the people walking along the dusty verges and the clouds of scarlet and blue flowers on the trees that lined the avenues.

This morning, though, he stared straight ahead, seeing nothing. He wanted to find a really good hiding place and never come out of it again. He wanted to become invisible and float through the rest of the day as a disembodied wraith. Most of all, he wanted to be back home in England, elbowing his way onto the bus with Scott, shouting friendly insults at Matthew, drawing faces in the condensation on the window.

'Nearly there,' said his dad. 'Cheer up. They're not going to eat you.'

An army of butterflies was swooping around in Tom's stomach as Dad slowed the car down and turned in through a pair of big gates. Tom clutched his bag tightly over his lap to hide his offending bare knees. He had a plan ready. If no one else was wearing shorts, he'd simply refuse to get out of the car. He'd pretend to have a heart attack or a brain haemorrhage or something and make Dad drive him away.

Then he saw the first boy. He was wearing shorts and a green shirt, exactly like Tom's. And there was another, and another. A whole crowd of them. It was OK. Tom was going to look OK. He'd never get used to this crazy uniform, but at least he wouldn't look like a total weirdo.

Simon wound down his window and called out to a woman who was walking up the drive towards the long low school buildings.

'Is the office up here somewhere?' he said.

The woman bent down to look into the car and saw Tom.

'Are you new?' she said. 'Is this your first day?'

Tom nodded dumbly. The woman smiled at Simon.

'Don't worry. I'll take care of him.'

Simon smiled back.

'Can you? Thanks. I'm late for work already.'

He turned to Tom and for a minute Tom was scared he'd say something embarrassing, or, even worse, hug him, but all he said was, 'Go on, hop out. Good luck.'

He put the car into gear. Tom was suddenly desperate for him to stay.

'Are you going to collect me after school?' he said.

'No. Didn't Mum explain? The school bus comes right to the end of our road. It'll drop you off.'

Tom fumbled with the door handle and Simon leaned across him and opened it.

'Give 'em hell,' he whispered. 'Show 'em who's boss.'

'Well now, what's your name?' the woman said brightly, as Tom walked beside her up the path towards a row of single storeyed classrooms behind deep verandahs.

'Tom Wilkinson.'

'Ah yes. You're going to be in Mrs Patel's class.' She beckoned to a boy standing with a group of others. 'Hassan, this is Tom. He's going to be in your class. Look after him till the bell goes. Show him where to go.'

It was the longest morning Tom had ever spent in his life. He felt like an alien, transported to another planet. Nothing was the same as it had been at home. The other kids weren't unfriendly, exactly, but they didn't have anything to say to him. There was no point in going on about Aston Villa, or his favourite TV programmes, which he and Scott always used to discuss at length. No one here would know what he was talking about.

There were a couple of others in his class who seemed to be English, quite a few who were

African or Asian, and one or two Americans or Canadians, but there were lots with names he'd never heard before. He heard one girl tell another something about 'back home in Madagascar', wherever that was, and there was a boy who couldn't speak much English, who Tom thought might be Italian.

I'll never get to be mates with this lot, he thought dismally, as he sat at his desk beside the window and gazed out over the huge sports field, which shimmered under the bright morning sun, while the maths lesson passed right over his head.

He began doing a complicated calculation, surreptitiously scribbling down the numbers in the margin of his notebook, trying to work out how many hours there were in two years, which was the time he'd have to spend here before he could go home. He was on the third or fourth try when the classroom door opened and the woman who'd brought him up from the car park walked in. The class jumped to their feet.

'It's Miss Hancock, the PE teacher,' the girl behind him whispered.

Tom's heart lurched. He was afraid she was going to say something about him.

'Sit down, everyone,' said Miss Hancock. 'I've come to tell you that the far end of the games field is out of bounds until further notice. The gardener found a pair of cobras there this morning, but they got away before he could catch and kill them.'

An involuntary gasp escaped from Tom. Miss Hancock heard it and turned to look at him.

'Don't worry, Tom,' she said. 'Snakes are more frightened of you than you are of them. When you've been here for a month or two you'll get used to this kind of thing.'

Tom sank back into his seat, his face scarlet. He looked surreptitiously round the class. The biggest boy, whose name was Pieter, was smirking and digging the boy next to him in the ribs.

I must watch out for him, thought Tom. I'd better be careful with him.

A bell rang soon after. It was lunchtime. The class spilled out noisily into the yard between the classrooms.

'The dining room's up there,' said Hassan, pointing towards a big hall further up the hill. He was obviously still feeling responsible for Tom, but he wanted to go off with his friends.

'I'll find it. Thanks,' mumbled Tom.

He pushed his hands into the pockets of his shorts, trying to look unconcerned, and went up the hill, following the others. Then he saw Afra. She was standing beside a noticeboard in the centre of a group of girls, arguing with one of them. He slowed down, hoping to catch her eye. It would be good to feel that at least one person recognized him, even if she hadn't been particularly friendly the other day in the forest. But Afra didn't see him.

'Yes,' he heard her say crossly, 'but just because a cobra's poisonous doesn't mean we have the right to go round killing them all, does it? Why can't they just take them someplace else?'

'Come on, Afra,' the other girl said. 'You don't mean you wouldn't kill a snake even if it was coming to get you and its fangs were dripping with poison and you knew you'd be dead in six minutes flat if it bit you? I mean that's just crazy.'

Afra's head tilted to one side and Tom caught a glimpse of her sudden smile.

'OK, if it was about to bite me, I guess I'd go for the self-preservation thing. But . . .'

'And you can't expect people to play games and everything on the games field when it's littered with five-metre long cobras and they've got to dodge about between them all the time?'

'There were only two of them, Rachel, and they were . . .'

Tom was beginning to feel embarrassed, standing on his own looking at a crowd of girls. He started walking on slowly up the hill. Cobras on the games field! he thought. Wow! Wait till Scott hears about this!

The path to the upper part of the school wound round a bushy area. Tom eyed it uneasily.

I'd pass out if I came face to face with a cobra,

he said to himself, shuddering. I'd try to run a mile first though.

'Tom!' He heard a shout behind him and looked round. Pieter, the big boy from his class, and his two friends were running up to him.

'Want to play cricket with us?' Pieter panted. He was holding something in his cupped hands.

Tom was pleased. He'd expected trouble from Pieter, not friendliness.

'Great. Yeah. Thanks,' he said.

'Here's the ball then. Catch,' said Pieter.

Tom held out his hands, but just in time looked up and caught the over-eager, expectant look in Pieter's face. He dropped his hands at exactly the same moment that Pieter opened his to drop something into them.

A long, thin, living thing fell to the ground. Warning bells rang in Tom's head.

Snake! he thought.

His instinct was to turn and run but he forced himself to stand still. This was a test, he knew. He had to pass it if he was to make his way in his class and in this school. Summoning all his courage, he stepped closer to the thing and bent down to look at it.

It was a kind of millipede, black and about fifteen centimetres long. Hundreds of short legs hung in a kind of curtain from each side of its round tubular body and rippled over the ground as it tried to hurry away.

'You've got to touch it. You've got to pick it up,' said a voice inside his head. 'They won't expect you to do that.'

He crouched down, pretending to admire it.

'Wow,' he said.

It can't be poisonous, he was telling himself, or Pieter wouldn't have held it in his hands in the first place.

Quickly, before he had time to change his mind, he reached down and picked the thing up. It curled up into a kind of knot in his palm. He found he didn't mind it after all. He didn't want to hurt it, either.

'Here you are,' he said, holding it out to Pieter. 'Weird kind of cricket ball. A bit soft, if you ask me.'

Pieter's eyes flickered.

'Nothing soft about chongalulus,' he said. 'They're armour plated. They haven't come here from abroad, like some foreign cissies.'

A knot was tightening inside Tom's stomach. He put the chongalulu down and it scuttled away to the shelter of a nearby bush.

'Good at running away, too, aren't they?' he said and he turned and walked slowly away, as casually as he could, towards the dinner hall.

He was nearly there when he heard footsteps running after him, and he braced himself as he turned, afraid of being tackled to the ground. The boy behind him was Richard, one of the group

38

that had been hanging round Pieter. He was smiling.

'You didn't mind the chongalulu then?' he said a little nervously.

'Chonga what?' said Tom.

'Chongalulu. That's what we call them. Mrs White nearly died of terror when we put one in her desk last term. I thought her eyes were going to pop right out of her head. You going up to the dining hall? I'll show you where to go if you like.'

Tom sat on the school bus on the way home in a daze of exhaustion. He felt as if a year, not a day, had passed since he'd come through the school gates that morning. He was stiff too and his legs were aching. There'd been sports all afternoon. He'd been playing football, keeping carefully to the snake-free end of the games field. Everyone was so fit here. They all seemed to be able to run fast and do brilliant headers and tackles. He'd always been good at football at home, but he was nothing special here.

He'd seen Afra getting onto the bus. He didn't go and sit next to her, but he was pleased she was there.

At least I'll know when I'm supposed to get off, he thought.

He was gazing vacantly at the trees, passing in a blur outside the window, when he felt someone touching his arm.

'You planning on staying on this bus all night?' Afra said.

He hoisted his bag up onto his shoulder and followed her to the door of the bus. Together they began to walk along the road.

'Listen, Tom,' Afra began. She stopped. Two women carrying bundles on their heads were waving and smiling at her from the other side of the road.

'Eh, Afra,' one of them called out. 'You are going home? We will walk with you. We want to visit Sarah.'

Afra clutched Tom's arm.

'Meet me by the stream in an hour,' she said. 'I've got to talk to you.'

Then she ran across the road to the two waiting women and disappeared through the overgrown gateway of the house next door to Tom's.

5

TIGER

Tom walked round the side of the house and let himself in through the back door that opened straight into the kitchen. He dumped his bag on the floor and went over to the fridge.

His mum came into the kitchen.

'Tom, don't leave your bag right there,' she said. 'Somebody'll fall over it and break their neck. Me, probably.'

Irritated, Tom kicked the bag into the corner of the room.

'I'm hungry,' he said. 'Where are the biscuits?'

'By the fridge, over there,' said Debbie. 'I haven't got the cupboards organized yet. Don't take too many. Watch what you're doing with that milk carton. Look, you're dripping it all over the floor.'

Without a word, Tom marched over to the sink, fetched out the floor cloth from under it, wiped the floor, put the cloth back, picked up his glass of milk and made for the kitchen door.

'Tom, where are you going?' said Debbie. 'You haven't told me about how you got on at school. Was your uniform all right?'

'Yes,' said Tom.

'I told you it would be. What's your new teacher like?'

'OK.'

'What about the other kids?'

'They're OK.' Tom put his glass of milk down on the table. 'There was this boy called Pieter. I thought he was going to . . .'

Bella came into the room trailing a blanket. Her face was red and bleary and she was sucking her thumb.

'Come here, Bella, come to Mummy,' said Debbie, holding out her arms. 'Did you wake up? Clever girl, to come downstairs all by yourself.'

Tom picked his milk up again, went out of the room and let the door slam behind him. At home he'd always flopped down for half an hour after he got in from school, and watched cartoons on TV. He'd sit on the floor and lean against the sofa and Tiger would curl up in his lap and purr so loudly that . . .

Tiger! Where was Tiger?

A cold feeling spread through Tom's stomach. Tiger had always been waiting for him in the kitchen when he'd got home in England. Why hadn't she been there today? What if she'd gone down to the stream again on her own, and the leopard had . . .

He put his milk and biscuits down on the bottom stair and dashed into the sitting room.

'Tiger!' he called out. 'Here, Tiger! Where are you? Mum, have you seen Tiger?'

There was no high-pitched miaow in response, no patter of paws on the shiny polished floor. Tom ran out of the room and up the stairs. He flung open the door of his bedroom. There was no black bundle of fur curled up on his bed, or lying stretched out on the heap of clothes he'd tossed into the corner of the room. He ran into Bella's room, then his parents', then the spare room which was still full of sealed-up boxes.

Tiger wasn't there.

He ran downstairs and searched in every corner.

'Tiger, I'm sorry,' he kept saying under his breath. 'I should have told Mum about the leopard. I should have told her to keep you in all day. I just didn't want them to know about the gap in the hedge. I'm sorry. I'm so sorry . . .'

He was standing in the middle of the sitting room now, fighting back tears. Then, out of the corner of his eye, he saw a movement. Tiger was outside on the verandah, lying on one of the basketwork chairs in the dappled shade made by the vine overhead.

Tom wrenched open the verandah doors, darted forward and snatched her up. He carried her inside and shut the doors again.

'You mustn't set foot outside again,' he said severely. 'Not while that leopard's around.'

He was trembling. Tiger sensed that something was wrong and struggled out of his arms. She stalked out of the sitting room, her tail held high. Tom followed her and found her sniffing at his milk and biscuits at the bottom of the stairs. He picked them up and took them back into the sitting room, sank down onto the floor and pointed the remote control at the TV.

A blast of unfamiliar music hit the room and the screen was filled with Africans dancing.

Of course, thought Tom. They won't have the same kind of programmes as we do at home.

He watched for a while, mesmerized by the costumes, the compelling rhythm and the energy of the dancers, but then they disappeared and a newscaster came on, talking in a language Tom didn't understand.

He leaned forward to look through the pile of videos beside the TV. They were mostly Bella's.

'Tom and Jerry,' he said out loud. 'This'll do.'

He put the cartoon into the video and started it. He'd seen it dozens of times before, but he didn't care. He sat back against the sofa drinking his milk, letting his hand wander to and from the packet of biscuits. Tiger, aware that he was relaxing now, crept into his lap.

'Shut up all that purring,' said Tom contentedly, stroking the cat in her favourite place under her chin. 'I can hardly hear the TV.'

Ten minutes passed. Then his mother came into the room.

'Bit stuffy in here, isn't it?' she said, going over to the verandah doors and opening them.

She stepped out and stood for a moment, looking down the garden.

'I thought being in Africa we'd be roasted alive,' she said, 'but you can't say it's too hot. I mean the weather's perfect, really.'

Tom wasn't listening to her. He was waiting for the huge pile of cans that Jerry had built up to topple over onto Tom's nose. But Tiger had heard Debbie's voice. She slipped out of Tom's arms, stretched herself and trotted out onto the verandah where she began to wind herself round Debbie's feet.

Tom suddenly realized that she'd gone. He jumped up and darted out to pick her up, then went back in and started to shut the verandah doors.

'What are you doing that for?' said Debbie.

Tom looked round, hunting for an excuse.

'It . . . it's those flowers on that creeper thing,' he said. 'They're making my nose itch.'

Debbie came back inside and closed the doors properly after her.

'You're not developing hay fever, are you?' she said. 'Your Uncle Paul started it at your age. It's been a real curse all his life.'

She began to go out of the room, then thought of something and turned back.

'Did you meet a girl called Tovey at school?'

Tom pretended to think.

'No,' he said. 'Why?'

'They live next door in that awful old bungalow. One of our neighbours popped in this morning. Mrs Musyoki. She's really nice. Really friendly. Her husband's a dentist. They're . . . Are you listening, Tom?'

The TV screen went blank as the cartoon finished. Tom watched it idly. He had pricked up his ears at the mention of the Toveys, but he wasn't interested in Mrs Musyoki, whoever she might be.

'Yes, I'm listening,' he said. 'The people next door are dentists and they're really nice.'

'No!' said Debbie. 'Honestly. The Musyokis live over the road, not next door. But Mrs Musyoki, her name's Beatrice actually – funny, really, you wouldn't expect an African to be called Beatrice, I don't know why – anyway, she told me that the Tovey people are really strange. The father's hardly ever there, and no one's ever seen the mother, and there's a little girl who runs completely wild, quite out of control, apparently, and the place is full of wild animals. There's another child, a boy called Joseph – I don't know how he fits into it all – but I'm not having you getting mixed up with them, Tom.'

Tom hunched his shoulders irritably.

Typical, he thought. That's so typical.

'Beatrice says the house is a real tip, not seen a lick of paint for donkey's years,' Debbie went on. 'And the garden's a total jungle. I had a look out of the window in your bedroom and she's right. What a mess! Just our luck to get awful neighbours.' She turned her head to listen and raised her voice. 'All right, darling! Mummy's coming! There's some paper right beside the toilet.'

Tom rolled over, tipping Tiger off his lap. He looked at his watch. Half an hour to go before he met Afra. It was a nuisance, Mum taking against the Toveys like that. It meant he'd have to be a bit clever and think of ways of getting round her. He'd done it before, often, but he didn't like doing it much.

I wish things didn't get so complicated, he thought.

What he really wanted was to go back down to the stream and see if he could find the leopard, see if there really was a leopard there. He hadn't quite believed Afra. Come to think of it, he hadn't quite believed in the cobras on the games field, either.

In spite of the strangeness of it all – the trees, the grass, the buildings – everything looked too normal to harbour such exotic hidden dangers, such wild things.

He had almost decided to go up to his room

and take a look out of the window at Afra's house next door when Bella trotted into the room, trailing something behind her. Tom had been lying quietly on the floor and she obviously hadn't expected to see him. The satisfied expression on her face disappeared and an anxious, furtive look came over her face. She turned and ran towards the door again, and Tom saw that she was holding Crocker by the neck.

He leaped up and darted over to her.

'I never goed in your room. I never . . .' she began.

He knelt down beside her, and opening his eyes as wide as they would go, stared into hers.

'If – you – ever – touch – Crocker – again,' he whispered, drawing his lips back from his teeth, 'a leopard will come out of the bushes and get you. It'll eat every little bit of you, starting with your nose. And it will *hurt*.'

Bella dropped Crocker as if he was made of red-hot metal and opened her mouth, her eyes round with horror. For a second Tom felt sorry, afraid he'd gone too far and scared her silly, but then she took a deep breath, and as she gathered herself for a truly spectacular scream, Tom felt nothing but disgust. Already aggrieved at all the trouble that was about to come down on his head, he snatched up Crocker, threw him right up onto the top of a high shelf beside the fireplace, and ran out through the verandah doors, shutting them carefully behind him.

It would make sense to disappear for a while. With any luck, by the time he came back from the stream, Bella would have stopped yelling and Mum would have forgotten all about it.

6

EYES IN THE SHADOWS

It's weird, thought Tom, as he bent double to follow the path beyond the fence. This is only the second time I've been here but it feels as if it's my own place, as if I'd been here hundreds of time before.

He was still scared, but it was a different kind of fear. Somehow, holding the chongalulu at school had helped. It had looked deadly, but had been harmless. It had given him more confidence.

Now, though, he was afraid of the leopard. He still didn't quite believe in it, partly because he didn't see how Afra could have really known it was there, and partly because it seemed so fantastic, so incredible, that such a dangerous, big, *wild* creature could be living somewhere as ordinary as the bottom of his garden. Even so, he looked intently into every shady hollow as he passed.

He stepped out into the glade and looked up and down the stream. No one was there. He was disappointed. He hadn't realized that he'd been looking forward to seeing Afra again.

I wonder where the monkeys are? he thought.

The silence was heavy, almost uncanny. Not even a breath of wind stirred in the trees or rattled the dead leaves on the ground. The only sound was the faint gurgling of the stream.

He had an odd feeling that he was being watched.

There was a big tree near the stream. Its crown rose in luxuriant clumps of glossy green leaves but its trunk was bare to the height of three or four metres.

Something was caught in the cleft where it divided. Something was dangling down.

Tom jumped across the stream, balancing on the stones that protruded from the water and looked up into the tree. All that was left of the dikdik hung limply from the branch. The tiny black hooves hung down pathetically from the torn legs. The head, horribly mangled, was hanging from a shred of hide.

Tom stepped back. This place was beginning to scare him.

There is a leopard then, he thought. It's real.

He saw the dikdik again in his mind's eye, remembering the way the sunlight had caught the hairs on its delicate ears, and its eyes, wide and luminous with fear.

That could have been Tiger, he thought with a shudder, and he pushed out of his mind a horrible vision of lifeless black paws and a tangle of fur clotted with . . .

I'm in danger here, he muttered. It might go after me.

He could feel the hairs on his head stand up. He was frighteningly alone.

He ran back to the stream. He was halfway across it, balancing on a rocky stone, when Afra came down the path into the glade. A wave of relief flooded over him. The crackle of fear all around subsided. The stream looked like a normal stream again, in a normal woodland.

'I didn't scare the dikdik off, if that's what you're thinking,' he said defensively. 'So you don't need to get mad with me.'

She grinned.

'I wasn't going to. I'm glad to see you, if you really want to know. It's why I came.'

He was pleased.

'We shouldn't hang around here,' he said. 'It's dangerous. The leopard got the dikdik. Look.'

He pointed to the pathetic tangle of hide and hooves in the tree. Afra drew in her breath sharply and started to jump across the stream, and he turned and hopped back with her. Together they went to the tree and looked up into it.

'That's what leopards do,' said Afra. 'They use trees like closets. Keep their food up there.'

Her eyes moved up the trunk into the thick crown of dark green leaves. Tom looked up too. It was difficult to make out anything because the light, where it pierced through the thick canopy of leaves, was so bright, and the shade was so deep. But then Tom saw it. There *was* something up there – a patch of shade denser than the rest.

Then he saw something else. A long, thin thing like a spotted rope was hanging down from the block of shadow.

At that moment, as if his eyes had clicked into focus, Tom saw the leopard. Afra had seen it at the same moment and her hand grabbed his arm.

The leopard lay at his ease on a branch in a regal pose, his head held high, his forepaws tucked under his chest. His golden eyes stared down, and in his face Tom saw an almost unbearable nobility, lonely and remote. He couldn't move. He could hardly breathe.

The leopard didn't like being watched. He was becoming uncomfortable. He blinked and moved his head uneasily to one side, turning his eyes away. Then he opened his mouth, threw his head back and yawned, and Tom caught a glimpse of two long curved canine teeth and the huge red tongue between them.

The leopard uncurled its forelegs as if it was going to sit up, and a stab of fear ran through Tom.

'It's coming down!' he whispered to Afra.

She had felt the fear too. She was already backing away towards the stream.

'Don't run,' she said softly in his ear. 'It'll make him want to chase after us. Back off slowly.'

They crossed the stream and began to walk cautiously up the path, looking over their shoulders constantly at the tree, but nothing moved in the high branches.

They turned a corner, and broke into a run, stumbling on the stones, ignoring the thorny vines that tore at their clothes.

Too late, Tom realized that he'd passed the clump of red-hot pokers, the plant that marked the way back home.

'I've come too far,' he panted. 'I've got to go back.'

'Don't,' said Afra. 'We're at my place. Look.'

Ahead was a chain link fence, much older than the one surrounding Tom's garden. It was rusty and holed in many places. Beyond it, the mass of unkempt trees and bushes wasn't much different from the tangle of undergrowth in the forest. There was no barrier here to keep a leopard out, but strangely it looked safe inside the fence, as if the chain link exerted a magical force that would keep danger at bay. Tom stepped through it with a shudder of relief.

'I shouldn't be here really,' he said. 'My mum doesn't know where I am. She'll kill me.'

But he didn't dare go back into the forest alone, and he couldn't resist seeing what lay on the far side of the bushes. He followed Afra down the well-trodden path that came out suddenly on to a patch of grass surrounded by tall trees, beyond which lay a long ramshackle bungalow.

An African boy was sitting under a tree, nursing a bulge under his red sweatshirt. He looked up when he heard Afra's footsteps.

'Where have you been? I have been waiting for you. Did you find that boy?'

'Yes, he's here,' said Afra. 'Listen, Joseph. You're not going to believe this. There *is* a leopard. We saw it. Tom and I saw it. It killed the dikdik and left it up a tree. It was up at the top, looking down at us.'

Joseph whistled. He looked past Afra, saw Tom and smiled. Then he leaned forward and gently pulled back his sweatshirt to let a big grey gosling tumble out onto the grass. It gave a squawk, waddled over to Afra and began to nuzzle her feet tenderly with its beak.

'Stumpy!' said Afra, bending down to stroke its back.

The boy stood up and shook a couple of downy smoke-coloured feathers off his shorts. He was taller than Tom.

'You are Tom?' he said.

'Yeah,' said Tom. 'Hi.'

'I'm Joseph.'

He spoke clearly, but Tom could tell that English wasn't his first language. Afra walked over to look at Stumpy's food bowl. The gosling waddled after her, lurching comically from side to side.

'Stumpy thinks Afra is his mama,' said Joseph, smiling at Tom. 'Where she goes, he always follows after her. You saw the leopard? You yourself?'

Afra picked the gosling up and caressed it gently.

'Yes,' said Tom. 'Funny thing was, before she – Afra – arrived I felt something was watching me. It must have been the leopard.'

He shivered.

'They'll hunt it,' said Joseph. 'They'll try to shoot it.'

'Who?' asked Tom.

'The people round here,' said Afra. 'Some of them have guns.'

'Guns? Why?' asked Tom.

Afra shrugged.

'For protection. Some of these guys even get a gun licence so they can shoot birds. Can you believe it?'

'But they wouldn't be allowed to shoot a leopard, would they?' said Tom. 'I mean, aren't leopards protected or anything?'

'They are, of course,' Joseph nodded, 'but these people don't care. They're frightened because of their cats and dogs.'

'Yeah, well, OK,' said Tom, thinking of Tiger. 'I don't blame them.' He felt confused. He couldn't bear to think of anything hurting Tiger, but at the same time he hated to think of the life being shot out of the proud, beautiful leopard.

'Did you tell anyone about it?' said Afra, turning on Tom with sudden fierceness. 'Did you tell your folks?'

'No,' said Tom. The way Afra was holding Stumpy made him think of Tiger again. 'But I ought to. They ought to know. It might get our cat.'

'You mustn't tell!' said Afra vehemently. 'You mustn't tell anyone!'

'That's what *you* say,' said Tom, feeling hassled, 'but what about my cat?' He paused. 'And my sister, too, come to think of it.'

'Yes, and what about my goose, and my bush-baby, and . . .'

'What bushbaby?'

'The leopards were here first,' Afra swept on, ignoring him. 'They have the *right* to be here. You just have to protect your cat. Lock her up at night, like I lock Stumpy up. Don't let her go too far.'

'Mummy! Mummy!'

From behind the mass of shrubs that divided the Toveys' garden from his, Tom heard Bella's voice.

'Mummy, I want you!'

'Is that your little sister?' said Joseph.

'Yes,' whispered Tom. 'I'll have to go. They don't know I'm here.'

'Hello-o! Debbee!'

Another voice came floating over the bushes.

'That's Mrs Musyoki,' said Joseph in a soft voice. 'She lives opposite us. Does she know your mother?'

'She met her this morning, I think,' said Tom.

'Oh, Debbie,' Mrs Musyoki was saying. 'I rang your doorbell but you didn't hear me. Sorry to disturb you, but . . . Oh!' Her voice became warm and soft, and even though they couldn't see her, the three listeners knew she must be smiling. 'Is this your little girl? Hello, darling. Come and say hello to auntie!'

Tom pulled a face and pretended to be sick.

'Where's your son, Debbie?' said Mrs Musyoki. 'Hasn't he come back from school yet?'

Debbie laughed.

'Tom? Oh, he's up in his room. I'd like to think he's doing his homework, but I'm sure he isn't. You know what boys are like at that age.'

'I just came over to ask if you'd seen my dog,' said Mrs Musyoki. 'It's a Jack Russell. His name is Tricky. I've called and called to him all afternoon but he doesn't come.'

'A Jack Russell?' said Debbie. 'No, I haven't seen any dogs around here at all. Don't worry. I'm sure it can't be far away. What harm could it come to, after all?'

7

AFRA'S HOUSE

Like the Wilkinsons' house next door, the Toveys' bungalow had a deep verandah, but the likeness ended there. Big terracotta flower pots stood on the Toveys' steps, from which lush plants with pale leaves sprouted luxuriantly. There was no smart new basketwork furniture on the Toveys' verandah. The chairs were ancient, with worn cushions whose once bright colours had faded to soft greens and blues. They looked inviting and deep and very comfortable. A ragged hat lay on one of them, and in the corner was a jumble of old tennis racquets and big stripy sun umbrellas.

The verandah's solid tiled roof was held up at the front by a couple of wooden posts which branched near the top. As they passed one of them, Joseph and Afra stopped and looked up at the angle in the post. Tom looked up too, and saw that a nest had been built there, and, sticking out of it, was a pair of little legs, each ending in a kind of foot with delicate toes and knobbly joints. A long furry tail was hooked comfortably over a nearby peg in the verandah post.

'What is it?' said Tom.

Joseph smiled down at him.

'A bushbaby,' he said. 'Afra found him when he was very small. Maybe his mother's dead, maybe he fell out of his nest. He's big now.' He tapped gently against the post. 'Hey! Kiksy!' he said.

'Kiksy? Is that his name?' said Tom.

'It's Kikombe, really,' said Afra. 'It's Swahili.'

The legs twitched for a moment but relaxed again. Afra stretched up and tickled one of the tiny feet. It jerked, and a little face appeared. Huge, reproachful eyes blinked down at her, and a pair of big round ears quivered. The bushbaby put his head on one side enquiringly, as if wondering what to do next, then the little head disappeared as he flopped down again on to his nest, rearranged his tail, and resumed his afternoon sleep.

'He only wakes up at night,' said Afra. 'It's a bit early for him still.'

They went on into the house. Tom looked around in amazement at the sitting room. He'd never seen so many books, except in a library, in his life. They lined the walls on shelves, covered the low table in front of the fireplace, and over-flowed in piles on the polished woodblock floor.

Afra flung herself down on a sofa. The springs sighed under her weight.

'OK, guys,' she said. 'What are we going to do?'

'That's easy,' said Joseph. 'There's only one thing we *can* do.'

'What?' said Tom.

'We can . . .' began Joseph. Then he stopped. A loud musical humming was coming from the other side of the door at the end of the sitting room.

'Mama,' said Joseph.

'Sarah,' said Afra.

The door opened, and in came the woman that Tom had seen from his bedroom window. She was not looking pleased.

'Afra! Where have you been?' she said, crossing her plump arms across her generous bosom. 'I been looking for you everywhere. Your dad call you up just now from Kampala. He want to know . . .'

Afra bounced up from the sofa.

'Prof? He called me? Is he going to call again?'

'Not today. His conference is very busy. He give a big lecture tonight, then . . .' She suddenly noticed Tom who was still standing by the door. 'Eh, who are you?'

'That's Tom,' said Afra carelessly. 'He's from next door. He just moved in here.'

'Nice to see you, Tom,' nodded Sarah. 'You kids are hungry? You want some of my cookies?'

'I don't think there are any.' Afra was looking a little nervously at Sarah. 'Yesterday I . . . We . . .'

'I know.' Sarah smiled. 'You two eat the whole tin.'

'And Kiksy,' said Joseph opening his eyes to make them look huge like the bushbaby's.

'That Kikombe!' Sarah said scornfully. 'He cannot eat more than three or two crumbs. Don't you try and blame that bushbaby! Anyway, it doesn't matter. I make fresh cookies today.'

Joseph was already on his way to the kitchen, dodging round his mother's large figure. She caught hold of him.

'Let me see these hands, now,' she said suspiciously. 'You been brooding Stumpy? You wash them before you touch my cookies.'

She smiled at Tom.

'Don't be shy,' she said. 'It is nice to see you. We are neighbours. You kids can all be good friends. Your mum and dad, they are OK? They need anything, they just come and . . .'

In the next room, a telephone rang.

'Prof!' cried Afra, starting towards the door. Tom heard her pick up the receiver, and say, 'Prof? Is that you?' then her voice went flat and she said, 'No, it's Afra here. You want Sarah? Hold on. I'll get her.'

'It's for you,' she said to Sarah, coming slowly back into the room.

'Must be the Reverend,' said Sarah, 'about Leah's baby,' and she went into the next room and shut the door.

Joseph came back with the open tin of cookies and sat down next to Afra on the sofa.

'Now, this is what we're going to do,' he said.

'Hadn't we better talk somewhere else?' said Tom. 'Won't she hear us?' He jerked his head towards the door.

Joseph and Afra burst out laughing.

'Once Sarah's on the phone,' said Afra, 'a volcano could erupt right there in the same room and she wouldn't notice a thing. Go on, Joseph.'

'OK.' Joseph offered the tin of cookies to Tom, but Tom shook his head. He wasn't sure enough yet about this house to eat anything in it. 'There's only two possible things that can happen,' Joseph went on. 'One is, the leopard stays here and it starts to eat people's cats and dogs. Maybe it's already eaten Mrs Musyoki's Jack Russell. If that happens, someone is going to get real mad and try to kill it. The other is, it's taken away, far away, to a game park where it can live in safety.'

'OK, sure, fine,' said Afra sarcastically. 'So how do we fix that? We lay a little trail of meaty bits along the road, all the way to Amboseli Park, and say, "Come on, kitty, come and—" '

'Afra, one day you are going to open your mouth so big an elephant is going to walk right into it,' said Joseph severely. 'We are going to tell my Uncle Titus.'

'But if we tell people,' said Tom anxiously, 'they'll come and shoot the leopard!'

'Not my Uncle Titus,' said Joseph. 'He works for the Kenya Wildlife Service.'

'Of course!' Afra waved her cookie in the air, scattering crumbs onto the brown wool rug. 'Why didn't I think of it before?'

'Because you are so busy opening your big mouth . . .'

'OK, wise guy.' Afra dug him in the ribs to shut him up.

'I still don't get it,' said Tom. 'How can your uncle get the leopard away from here without killing him?'

'He can get the translocation service,' said Joseph. 'They dart the leopard with anaesthetic drugs, and when he's asleep they put him in a cage and take him far away, to Amboseli, maybe. Or Meru.'

'Great,' said Afra, becoming businesslike again. 'Have you got his number, Joseph? Let's call him up now.'

Joseph shook his head.

'He's on safari,' he said. 'He went last week. Maybe he's away for two weeks, three weeks . . .'

'But we can't wait that long!' said Tom, thinking of Tiger. 'Don't you even know where he is?'

'Yesterday he was in Naivasha,' said Joseph. 'I know that because his office phoned Mama.'

'Well, can't we leave a message for him to phone us back?' said Tom.

'Yes, but we'd have to say why we were calling, and they'd realize we were kids and wouldn't take us seriously, and someone from his office would probably call back while we're at school, and tell Sarah there's a leopard prowling around the place, and she'd panic and . . .'

'He didn't phone, anyway,' said Joseph, stemming Afra's flow. 'He sent an e-mail from the office in Naivasha. They've got it working again. It wasn't good last month because a giraffe walked into the telephone lines.'

'Pity you're not on e-mail then,' said Tom. 'If you were . . .'

Afra jumped to her feet.

'But we are!' she said. 'At least, Prof is.'

'Afra, you cannot use Prof's e-mail!' Joseph looked scandalized. 'You know what happened last time you tried to do something with his computer. You messed up his files, and who got all the blame? I did.'

'Yes, but this is different. This is an *emergency*.'

'Anyway, Uncle Titus might be anywhere by now, way up north, I don't know. He won't have e-mail up there.'

'Yes,' said Afra eagerly, 'but we could send an e-mail to his office and ask them to radio the message on to him. They could do that, couldn't they? And they'd be more likely to take it seriously than a telephone message from a bunch of kids.' Her face clouded. 'There's only one problem. I don't know how to send e-mails.'

'I do,' said Tom. He sat back, basking in a

delightful sense of superiority, the first he'd felt since he'd met Afra. 'Where's your dad's computer, then? Let's do it now.'

Afra sat down again on the sofa.

'It's in there, in Prof's study,' she said, jerking her thumb towards the door behind which could be heard Sarah's voice answering the Reverend with soft *Eh, eh's*, and a liquid flow of Swahili.

'We must wait,' said Joseph.

'I can't wait for long,' said Tom. 'Mum'll be looking for me soon, for supper.'

'OK,' said Joseph. 'Don't worry.' He went to the study door and opened it. 'Mama!' he said. 'Come quick!'

There was no response.

'Mama!' he shouted, at full volume. 'There's a baboon in your vegetable patch!'

There was a click as the receiver went down and Sarah shot out of the study, moving fast on unexpectedly light feet.

'Go on, both of you,' said Joseph. 'I'll stay in here and keep her out of the study.'

'Where's the address?' said Tom.

'It's on the machine, in the address book,' said Joseph. 'I know because Professor sent a message to Uncle Titus once before. Hurry up! Maybe Mama will want to telephone the Reverend back again.'

Tom felt nervous, walking into Professor Tovey's study. There were even more books in here, and papers were scattered in piles every-where, on the desk, on the battered armchair under the window and even on the floor.

Afra marched across to the desk and flicked a switch on the computer. She looked out of the window and laughed.

'It's OK. I guess Sarah's going to be busy for a while yet. Look at her! Once she gets started pulling weeds she won't come in for anything.'

Tom was watching the screen, waiting for it to warm up, listening to Afra's voice. Something occurred to him.

'Why have you got an American accent?' he said.

'What do you mean?' said Afra. '*I* don't have an accent. *You* do. A British one.'

'No, I don't. *You* . . .' said Tom.

'Well, anyway,' said Afra, who could see the argument might go on for ever, 'if I have, it's because I am American, like Prof. I was born in Washington.'

'But you're mum's not American. Sarah's . . .'

'Sarah's not my mom, dumbo. She just looks after me. My mom came from Ethiopia.'

'Oh. Right. Is she there now?'

'Nope. She's dead.'

Tom felt embarrassed.

'I didn't know. I mean . . .'

'It's OK. Look, this thing's warmed up now. Let's send this e-mail, OK?'

Tom wasn't used to the Professor's software. He tapped at the keyboard nervously, afraid of doing something that would mess it up, while Afra kept her eye on Sarah, who was still busy in her vegetable patch.

'That's it. Got it,' he grunted at last.

'Got what?'

'Got the right screen up. OK, so what do you want me to say?'

Afra thought for a moment.

'How about this? "Dear Uncle Titus . . ." '

'He's not your uncle,' objected Tom.

'Don't interrupt. I've known him since I was born. I always call him that. "Dear Uncle Titus, We need to speak to you very urgently about a leopard . . ." no, delete leopard, "a certain predator . . ." '

'How do you spell predator?'

Afra peered at the screen.

'That looks OK to me, the way you did it,' she said doubtfully. 'OK – "a certain predator that we are afraid might start to get into trouble. We want to save it before someone takes the law into their own hands." '

'That sounds great,' said Tom.

' "So please contact us urgently, after 4 pm when we'll be at home. Don't speak to anyone around here about this." '

'Why not? You'll have to give him a reason.'

' "Don't speak to anyone around here about

this . . . um, for obvious reasons",' Afra finished triumphantly. 'Then put "Love from Afra and Joseph". And Tom, if you like.'

'No, he doesn't know me,' said Tom. 'That's it?'

'I guess,' said Afra, peering over his shoulder. 'Wait. I'll read it again.' She read, frowning at the screen, then straightened up and grinned. 'You type real well, Tom. You're so quick. OK, let's send it now.'

'There she goes!' said Tom, enthusiastically clicking the *Send Now* button. 'Wa-hey!'

The door opened.

'Ma's coming!' said Joseph. 'Hurry!'

Tom searched the screen, his fingers suddenly all thumbs, not quite knowing how to exit.

'Quick!' hissed Afra. 'Just turn it off!'

'You can't,' said Tom. 'It messes it up. I'm trying to . . . Yes, that's it. Come on, come on! Why does it do everything so slowly?'

They heard Sarah's feet on the verandah steps, then her voice, asking sharply, 'Why is Afra in Professor's study? I saw her from the garden.'

'Oh,' Joseph's voice was deliberately casual. 'She is just looking for something, Mama. A . . . pencil.'

'Afra got plenty of pencils of her own,' said Sarah, marching to the study door.

The door opened. The creak of the hinge masked the faint electronic sigh of the computer as the power faded from it. Afra and Tom had leaped across the room just in time and were gazing at a shelf covered with crumbling old shards of pottery. The early African night was already falling and it was getting too dark to see properly.

'If you are messing up Professor's stuff, Afra . . .' began Sarah.

'I'm just showing Tom his latest finds,' said Afra, looking virtuous. 'He's really interested, aren't you, Tom?'

Tom nodded his head vigorously. He had no idea why the Professor chose to keep a load of broken flower pots in his room, but he wasn't going to say a word.

Sarah looked at them suspiciously.

'Well . . .' she said, 'if you want to study, why you don't put on the light and . . .'

At that moment, something small and brown and furry hurtled through the air, leaping across the room to land on Afra's shoulder. Tom started back in alarm, and Sarah laughed at the expression on his face.

'That bushbaby is the best jumper I ever see in my life,' she said. 'You bring him out of here, Afra, before he gets the idea he can make a nest in your dad's papers.'

Kiksy was clinging lovingly to Afra's shoulder, making low hooting noises in her ear.

'Hey, Kiksy, you're tickling me,' said Afra,

putting up a hand to stroke the tiny creature's back.

Tom watched enviously. He wanted to feel the bushbaby on his own shoulder. He followed Afra out of the room and Kiksy swivelled his head round and stared at him, his enormous brown eyes pools of dark amber in his melancholy little face.

'He's hungry, for sure,' said Joseph.

'Well, he's not getting any cookies tonight,' said Afra. She nuzzled the bushbaby's neck with her nose. 'You have to go hunting yourself, Kiksy, do you understand? Catch yourself a nice juicy moth or two. You're not a bushbaby now. You're a bush adult. Nearly, anyway.'

Kiksy suddenly took another spectacular leap right across the sitting room to land on the curtain rail. He sat there with his tail hanging down, looking soulfully round the room.

'Time you went out to shut Stumpy in now,' said Sarah, going out of the room towards the kitchen, 'case some animal come and get him in the night.'

Tom, Joseph and Afra looked at each other in dismay.

'She doesn't know, does she?' said Tom.

'Nah, she just said it,' said Afra. 'Could have meant anything. A hyena, or a dog even.'

She went over to the standard lamp in the corner by the fireplace and switched it on. Soft

71

light flooded the room. It lit the tin of cookies lying open on the sofa. Absent-mindedly, Tom took one and bit into it. It was delicious. He realized that he was very hungry.

'It's late!' he gasped. 'I've got to go. Mum'll kill me!'

He ran out onto the verandah. Through a gap in the trees ahead, the Ngong hills appeared, lying like a streak of dark purple cloud along the horizon. Above them, the sky was already darkening to a deep inky blue. Tom paused. There was something he had to know before he ran home.

'Why does your dad keep all those broken flower pots in his room?' he asked Afra.

'Flower pots?' she laughed. 'They're not flower pots. They're archaeological finds, thousands of years old. Prof's an archaeologist.'

'Oh,' said Tom. 'I see.'

He began to run down the garden towards the holes in the fence.

'Don't go that way,' Afra called after him. 'The leopard hunts at night. Go up round the front and into your house by the road. See you on the school bus in the morning.'

'Yeah,' said Tom. 'See you.'

8

MORE TROUBLE WITH PIETER

Debbie hit the roof.

'Where *have* you been?' she said, her cheeks mottled pink with fury. 'What on *earth* have you been doing?'

'Sorry, Mum,' said Tom, surreptitiously wiping a cookie crumb off his shirt front. 'I just went out into the road. Thought I heard someone calling.'

'You've been gone for ages! I've been searching for you for the last fifteen minutes at least! You just don't think, do you? Anything might have happened. How do you know what . . .'

'I wasn't doing any harm. I only went out of the gate for a few minutes.' Tom was beginning to believe his own story. 'There was this boy. I got talking to him.'

'What boy?' Debbie stared at him suspiciously. 'You can't just start talking to people like that. They might be . . .'

Tom detected a chink in Debbie's logic.

'*You* started talking to Mrs Mus-whassername. She just came round here and . . .'

'Beatrice's husband did dentistry at Guy's hospital in London. They lived in England for years.'

'So?'

Tom felt he was getting the advantage. So did Debbie. She changed tack.

'Who was this boy, anyway?'

'His name's Joseph,' said Tom, deciding that the more truth he wove into his story the easier it would be to sustain it.

'Where's he from?'

'I don't know. He lives round here somewhere.'

'No, I mean, where's he *from*? Is he Kenyan, or English, or . . .'

'If you're trying to ask me if he's black or white, he's black,' said Tom, beginning to feel resentful on Joseph's behalf.

'Does he go to your school?'

'No. Maybe. I don't think so. What does it matter?'

'I'll tell you what matters. Beatrice says there's a terrible lot of crime round here, robbery, attacks, car hijacking . . .'

'Yeah, well I wasn't driving a car,' muttered Tom rebelliously.

Debbie's flush deepened.

'I won't have it, Tom, do you hear? I won't have you picking up total strangers, getting in with riff-raff, going out and . . .'

She stopped. Tom's face had frozen.

'You don't know anything about Joseph,' he burst out. 'You've got no right to call him names.

He's *nice*. I *like* him. We were talking about bush-babies.'

Debbie looked mystified.

'Wildlife,' Tom went on. 'He knows all about it.'

'Oh.'

Debbie looked a little mollified. There was a reassuringly educational sound to 'wildlife'.

Tom pressed his advantage.

'I've got to make friends, Mum,' he said. 'You always try and stop me. You didn't even like Scott at first. You wouldn't let me go round to his house for ages.'

'I didn't know the family,' said Debbie. 'They might have been . . .'

'Yes, but they weren't, were they? And think of all the times I could have . . .'

Debbie suddenly capitulated. She put an arm round Tom's shoulders and squeezed them.

'OK, love, I'm sorry. I know I get a bit het-up sometimes. It's only because I'm scared something awful will happen.'

'Yeah, well.' Tom tried to look dignified. 'I'm not a little kid any more. I'm thirteen.'

Debbie smiled. Tom wondered if she was laughing at him but decided not to take offence. He'd won the battle. There was no point in stirring things up again.

'Come on,' said Debbie. 'Come into the kitchen. Your supper'll probably be burned to a crisp by now. And listen, next time you want to disappear and give me a terrible fright, just warn me first, OK?'

The next morning, Tom sat silently over his breakfast. He was worried about Tiger. Afra had said something about leopards hunting at night. Did that mean they didn't hunt during the day? He calculated in his head how many hours he'd be away from home. Seven or eight, at least. Tiger certainly wouldn't stay indoors all that time.

'Mum!' he said suddenly.

Debbie had been spooning cereal into Bella's mouth. She turned and looked at him.

'What?'

'Don't let Tiger . . .' Tom began. Then he stopped. He couldn't ask Mum to keep Tiger indoors all day without giving her a reason, but if he gave her the real one, he'd break his promise to Afra and betray the leopard as well.

'Don't let Tiger what?' said Debbie.

Simon came into the room.

'You nearly ready, Tom?' he said. 'Got your PE kit?'

Tom remembered the PE lesson yesterday and the snakes on the field. Inspiration came to him.

'Don't let Tiger out today,' he said. 'That boy I told you about yesterday, Joseph, he told me he'd seen a snake in our front garden.'

'A snake!' Debbie gripped the back of Bella's

chair as if it might slip away from her. 'Where was it?'

'I didn't see it,' said Tom truthfully. 'All Joseph said was that it was in our front garden.'

'They asked me at the office if we wanted someone to do the garden,' Simon said. 'I wasn't sure if we'd need it, but I think I'd better tell them we do.'

Debbie was looking at him with panic in her eyes.

'What'll I do if it comes into the house?' she said. 'You've got to stay at home today, Simon! You can't go off and leave me on my own!'

'Don't be daft, Debs,' said Simon. 'I can hardly stay off work because my son met some kid who might or might not have seen a snake in the garden.'

'He said it was only a small one,' said Tom, feeling a little guilty.

'They're the worst!' cried Debbie. 'They're more likely to get in under the door! And anyway, the small ones are the most poisonous!'

'You'll be fine,' said Simon. 'The last people here never had any trouble with snakes. Just keep the doors shut, and if you go out, mind where you put your feet. And better not let Bella out into the garden.'

'Or Tiger,' said Tom.

'I'm not letting Bella out of my sight,' said

Debbie vehemently. 'Is that all you've got to say, Simon? How on earth . . .'

'Tom, get your stuff and come,' said Simon hastily. 'We're going to be late.'

'Watch out for Tiger, won't you, Mum?' said Tom, opening the back door, which Debbie was waiting to snap shut behind him.

Tom sat silently in the car. He wasn't ready for school. He wasn't ready for Pieter.

'What's the matter with you?' said Simon. 'Cat got your tongue?'

Tom didn't answer. Simon turned his head to look at a group of boys in St Peter's uniform who were walking up from the main road towards the school gates.

'Did you get any hassle yesterday?' he said.

Tom hesitated.

'Not a lot,' he said.

'Keep out of harm's way, that's my advice,' said Simon, stopping the car. 'Don't go looking for trouble, but if you've got to fight, give it everything you've got.'

Tom grunted non-committally as he opened the car door and got out.

What do you know about it, anyway? he thought to himself.

He kept out of Pieter's way, though, and got through the day all right. Pieter deliberately crashed into him in the doorway of the dining hall, and then apologized extravagantly, trying to make out that he thought Tom was a pathetic wimp who would burst into tears if his precious little nose was grazed; and no one particularly wanted to sit next to him at the dinner table; but on the other hand, a boy called Rajiv grinned at him in English and showed him the right page in the book, and another one called Paul lent him his ruler in Geography. He really wanted to see Afra, to ask if Joseph had heard from his uncle, but she was always with some other girls and he felt too embarrassed to go up to them.

I'll see her on the bus, anyway, he thought.

But when he climbed on to the bus at the end of another afternoon session of PE, the first face he saw was Pieter's. He was at the back with a couple of hangers-on.

'Oo!' Pieter called out as he saw Tom's head appear. 'Daddy doesn't take him home from school then, does he? He only brings him in the morning.'

Tom crossed his eyes, stuck out his tongue and waggled his ears. The other people on the bus laughed. Pieter scowled and said something to the boys beside him, who grinned and prodded each other.

Tom dropped into the empty seat beside Afra.

'What's he doing here?' he said. 'He wasn't on the bus yesterday.'

'He had a football match. He's in the team,'

said Afra. 'Didn't you know he lives right near us? Just along the street? He's a pain.'

'You don't have to tell me,' said Tom. 'Wow, that's all I need. Pieter Prince Charming Hoven on the bus every day.'

'Never mind him.' Afra unwrapped a candy bar and offered a chunk to Tom. 'Are you coming over to my place now? Maybe Uncle Titus is going to call.'

'I . . . can't.' Tom felt embarrassed. 'My mum went ballistic last night. She's really weird about . . . about people she doesn't know. I mean, she goes crazy if I hang out with anyone new.'

Afra looked at him suspiciously.

'Has she met anyone in our street yet?'

'Yes. Mrs Musyoki. Why?'

'Aha. That explains it. Mrs Musyoki has a real down on us. Thinks the Toveys are some kind of alien weirdos from the planet Mars. She never got over the time when Pumpkin (he was my weaver bird that I brought up from a chick till he flew away) got into her bedroom and made a mess on her pillow. I bet she's stuffed your mum full of garbage about how "the Toveys are so strange, and that poor little girl runs wild and you should see the mess in that house".'

Tom nodded in gloomy silence.

'Mum'll come round in the end,' he said. 'She's scared of everything because she's new here. She'll be OK.'

'But we've got to talk!' said Afra. 'We've got to be able to contact each other!'

'Yes, but how?'

Afra nodded decisively.

'I've got it. You know that jacaranda tree in your garden?'

'Jacaranda? What's that?'

'It's got blue flowers. It's right up close to our fence.'

'Oh, right. I know the one you mean.'

'Well, there's a place behind it which you can't see from your house and there's a way through the bushes on my side that goes right up to the fence. We can talk there. The only problem is, we won't know when the other person's there.'

'I know,' said Tom. 'We'll need a signalling system. There's a window in my bedroom that overlooks your garden.'

'The round one,' nodded Afra.

'Yes. Well, what if you tie a scarf or something round a tree where I can easily see it when you want to tell me something urgently? Then I'll go down to the fence to meet you.'

'But I might have to wait for hours,' objected Afra. 'You won't be looking out of your window all the time.'

'You can leave a note tucked into the fence, with a message on it, or giving me a time, like "Meet me at 6 o'clock". Then I'll think up an excuse to go into the garden to meet you.'

'Biology project,' said Afra. 'Collecting leaves and seeds. We're doing one. Aren't you?'

'I don't know,' said Tom. 'I haven't had Biology yet.'

The bus was slowing down. Tom and Afra stood up, ready to get off. Tom didn't look down towards Pieter at the far end, but he heard a burst of mocking laughter.

'Good thing he doesn't get off here,' he said to Afra, as they walked together up the road. 'I don't want that idiot living right on my doorstep.'

'He does, practically. He's in the next street along. His backyard runs down to our strip of forest on the other side.'

'Does he come into it much?' said Tom anxiously. He hated the thought of his special place being invaded by Pieter Hoven.

Afra laughed.

'Pieter? Are you kidding? His dad'd kill him. He never lets Pieter go anywhere. He's mean, Mr Hoven. Real mean.'

9

AFRA'S SIGNAL

Debbie was in a good mood when Tom walked in through the kitchen door.

'Guess what? Hamburgers for supper,' she said. 'I've found a really nice shopping centre near here. You can get practically anything. Imported stuff too – at a price, of course. Lise Hoven took me.'

Tom's hand had been halfway to the biscuit cupboard, but he dropped it and turned round sharply.

'Lise who?' he said.

'Hoven. They live just round the corner. Her husband is your dad's boss. I was quite nervous, really, meeting her, but she's a bit of mouse. Quiet and sort of timid. She says she's got a son at your school. Pieter, his name is. Have you met him yet?'

'Yes,' said Tom, turning back to the cupboard. 'Oh yes, I've met him.'

'You don't sound very keen.'

'He's a total prat, Mum. A complete and utter . . .'

'Oh darling, I'm sure he isn't that bad. Can't you make friends with him? Mr Hoven hasn't been all that . . . well, easy, so far, Dad says. Maybe if you and Pieter were friends . . .'

'I'd rather make friends with a rattlesnake,' said Tom, picking up the biscuits. The word 'rattlesnake' jogged his memory. 'Where's Tiger?'

'In the sitting room with Bella. She fell asleep, poor little thing, on the sofa cushions, practically on top of Tiger. Now don't go and wake her up, Tom. It's been difficult, I can tell you, keeping her indoors all day. She kept wanting to out into the garden like she used to at home, then she saw that old crocodile of yours up on the shelf and for some reason she got upset and started to scream and . . .'

'I'll go upstairs to my room,' said Tom guiltily. 'There's not much point in watching telly. I know all the videos we've got backwards anyway.'

'At least we'll be able to go out of doors tomorrow.' Debbie was walking round the kitchen, fetching out her chopping board and knife. 'Murchisons have found a man for us. He's going to do the garden, and if there are any snakes he's going to deal with them. Oh, and Beatrice says why don't we have a girl to help in the house? Everyone else does. It's quite a lot, I suppose, to manage on my own, and if it's as cheap as she says – but I've never had anyone like that before and I'm not sure if . . .'

Tom was already out of the kitchen door and halfway to the stairs.

Pieter Hoven, he thought, resisting the temptation to stamp on each tread in case he woke Bella. Just my luck that I've ended up in the same class.

Then he remembered Tiger. He hadn't seen her since he'd come home from school. He had to be sure that she was OK. He tiptoed downstairs again and opened the sitting room door. Tiger and Bella were asleep together on the sofa, a tangle of black fur and yellow curls. He felt a tinge of annoyance.

Tiger likes me best, I know she does, he told himself as he went upstairs.

As soon as he was in his room he jumped up onto his bed to look out of the round window, wondering which tree Afra would tie her scarf to.

There can't possibly be one yet, he thought. She won't even have had time to put her bag down, let along run round the garden tying scarves to trees.

He stepped down off his bed and opened his schoolbag. He wasn't going to do his homework yet, not till after supper, but there was a sweet at the bottom of the bag somewhere.

He found it, unwrapped it, put it in his mouth and dropped down onto the bed. There was a pack of cards on the windowsill by the bed. He picked them up and idly began to shuffle them. Then he switched on his radio alarm and pressed the tuning buttons, trying to find some decent music. He gave up after a moment or two, jumped up on his bed again and looked out through the round window.

It was there! The scarf was there, tied round a tree on the far side of the grassy patch, where he could see it easily.

She's got a message then, from Uncle Titus, he thought.

He went quietly down the stairs again and slipped out through the front door, doubled back down the side of the house and ran down to the jacaranda tree.

Afra was still there on the other side of the fence, trying to attach a note to the chain link. She looked up when she heard Tom coming.

'Great,' she said. 'It works. You saw the scarf OK?'

'Yeah, easy,' said Tom. 'You've heard from him then? From Uncle Titus?'

'He called, just as I was coming into the house. Lucky the bus wasn't late today.' Afra grimaced. 'It's not good news. He's away till Monday.'

'Did you tell him the predator was a leopard?'

'Yes. He said . . .'

'Can they take it away to a game park?'

'No. Will you shut up and listen? I'm trying to tell you.' She swallowed. 'He said leopards don't settle down too well in new places. They get fought off by the ones who are there already. It's really tough out there for them, Tom.'

'I know the feeling,' muttered Tom.

Afra didn't notice.

'He said . . . he said, if the leopard's started eating pets and hanging round houses, they won't have any choice. They're going to have to shoot him.'

Tom stared at her in disbelief. Afra and Joseph had been so certain that Uncle Titus would save the leopard, whisk him magically away to some leopard heaven where there'd be dikdiks under every . . . But he didn't want to think about the dikdik. He didn't want to remember the sad limp bundle hanging from the branch. It made him too scared for Tiger.

'Well,' he said slowly, 'if I have to choose between Tiger and the leopard, I suppose it would have to be Tiger.'

Afra grabbed the chain link and rattled it fiercely.

'No!' she said. 'You can't think like that! You mustn't! You saw him, Tom. You looked at him. You can't want him to die.'

Tom suddenly felt angry.

'I don't want him to be carted off to some place he doesn't like either,' he said, 'where he won't know where he is, and he'll get picked on by all the other leopards.'

'OK, but he's strong and young,' said Afra. 'Why can't he have a chance? Anyway, where did he come from before he came here? Maybe he could go back there. Maybe he'd try again and find someplace else, by himself, where he *wants* to be.'

'Oh yeah? And how do we do that? Like you said, lay a trail of little bits of meat and call out, "Come on, Kitty"?'

Afra shook her head.

'OK,' she said. 'No need to get sarcastic on me.'

'Tom! Afra!'

Joseph arrived, panting, at the fence.

'You look hot,' said Tom.

'I've been running,' said Joseph, dropping down to a squat while he got his breath back. 'Three miles back from school.'

'Why didn't you go on the school bus?' asked Tom.

Joseph looked unsmilingly at him.

'We don't have a bus at my school. All the pupils must walk. For me it's only three miles. For some it's much further.'

'But why don't you come to school with us?' said Tom.

'Because our school costs a lot of money,' said Afra, looking embarrassed. 'Why do you think there are so many white and foreign kids there, when this is an African country? It's a school for rich kids.'

Tom was puzzled.

'But my family's not rich,' he said. 'Not really. I mean at home . . .'

'At home's different,' said Afra impatiently. 'In

America, you're poor if you don't have a car. In Africa, you're rich if you have a decent pair of shoes.'

Tom felt ashamed.

'I'm sorry,' he said. 'I . . .'

Joseph stood up. He wasn't panting now. He looked down at Tom and smiled.

'This is an economic problem,' he said. 'Money is very nice, but it can't buy you everything. Anyway, I'm going to be a very rich man one day. I'm going to be a world-famous zoologist. Or a pilot.'

'And I'm going to be the man in the moon,' said Afra. 'Listen, Uncle Titus called.'

'He says they can't move the leopard,' said Tom quickly, glad to change the subject. 'The other leopards would all fight it.'

'They may have to shoot it,' said Afra, in a small voice.

'Shoot a leopard?' Joseph looked incredulous. 'But it's a protected animal. I don't believe that Uncle Titus said such a thing.'

'He did,' said Afra. 'Call him if you don't believe me.'

Joseph thought for a moment.

'How many cats and dogs has it eaten?' he said.

'We don't know for sure if it's eaten any,' said Afra, after a moment. 'Mrs Musyoki's Jack Russell went missing, but that doesn't mean the leopard ate it.'

'Why?' asked Tom. 'What difference does it make anyway?'

'If the leopard hasn't started hunting for domestic animals,' said Joseph, 'maybe he hasn't yet acquired the habit. Maybe he was hunting only for the dikdik, and when he found it and ate it, he was satisfied, and left back again for his old place.'

'You mean we'd better go and check if he's still there,' said Afra. 'When shall we go? Now?'

'Not just yet,' said Tom. 'I can't disappear again like I did yesterday. I have to have a reason.'

He thought for a moment, and a slow smile crossed his face.

'I've got it!' he said. 'I bet it works. If it does, I'll be round at your place again in a couple of minutes!'

10
DANGER!

Bella had woken up when Tom crept back into the house. She was sitting on the kitchen floor, playing with some plastic toys. She looked up anxiously.

'Did it come?' she said. 'That thing? What eats . . .'

'Mum,' said Tom, quickly. 'I'm going out for a bit. I've left my atlas at school and I can't do my geography homework. I just want to see if Pieter Hoven will lend me his.'

Debbie looked up, surprised, from the onion she was chopping.

'But I thought you didn't like Pieter?'

'I don't, much,' said Tom casually. 'He's OK, I suppose. Anyway, I need that atlas.'

He walked past her towards the back door and opened it.

'Tom! Stop!' said Debbie, coming to the kitchen door after him. 'You can't just barge in on people like that. I'll phone Lise and see if it's convenient.'

Tom turned round and came back.

'Mum, stop fussing,' he said irritably. 'Pieter was on the school bus with me. I know he's at home. I'll only be five minutes.'

'All right,' said Debbie doubtfully. 'But go straight there and come straight back, OK? And you'll be polite to Mrs Hoven. You know her husband's . . .'

'Dad's boss. You told me.'

Tom walked on towards the gate. The front garden of the house was quite deep, with a thick hedge of a spiky kind of bush separating it from the road. Tom went out through the gate, then looked back to check that Debbie had gone inside. She had. He didn't know which direction the Hovens' house was. He didn't want her to see him going the wrong way. He turned left, and dived through the entrance to the Toveys' garden.

Joseph and Afra were sitting on the steps of the verandah at the back of the bungalow while Stumpy dabbled contentedly among the old leaves by Afra's feet. They were arguing.

'Afra, listen to me,' Joseph was saying. 'Uncle Titus, he knows a lot about leopards. They've tried the translocation method. They've tried other kinds of solution. They've tried everything.'

'But to shoot him! It's just not right.' Afra had been absent-mindedly stroking Stumpy's silky back feathers, but she stopped and raised her face, hot with anger. 'They could at least give him a chance to . . .' She saw Tom and jumped off the bottom step. 'We were about to give up on you. Come on, let's go.'

They started off down the garden towards the

92

hole in the fence, Joseph leading the way while Stumpy waddled valiantly behind.

'Stumpy, no. Stay here,' Afra said, falling behind the others. 'It's too dangerous for you out there.'

'Afra!' Sarah came out onto the verandah. 'Where are you going? Come back here.'

'Why?' Afra called back. 'I have something real urgent to do.'

'Yes, and I have something more urgent for you to do.' Sarah was walking purposefully towards her. 'There is a hole in Stumpy's night cage. You leave him there tonight, and he will get out and who knows what will happen to him.'

'I'll do it later,' said Afra. 'Not right now. Please, Sarah.'

'And you have not fed him yet,' Sarah went on.

'Oh Sarah, please, couldn't you do it? Just this once?' wheedled Afra.

'No. Leah is coming with the baby. I will be too busy.'

'OK.' Afra knew she was beaten. She turned back to Tom and Joseph who had stopped to wait for her. 'You guys go on. I'll come later. Come, Stumpy.'

Tom slipped through the hole in the fence after Joseph and followed him down the path. He'd been feeling nervous about going back into the forest. He'd imagined the leopard stalking by the stream, its tail waving behind it, or crouched ready to spring, its spots making it invisible in the dappled shade, or lying watchfully up in a tree, as he had seen it the first time, waiting to drop down on any prey beneath in a flurry of fang and fur.

We're just meat on feet to leopards, he thought.

But the sight of Joseph's green-shirted back ahead, moving nimbly between the grasping thorny vines, was reassuring. Joseph didn't seem scared. He'd known this place all his life. He wouldn't be walking quite so confidently, surely, if he felt they were in immediate danger.

They came out into the glade. Ahead of them, on the far side of the stream, was the tree where the leopard had been before. Tom had been expecting to see the dikdik remains up the tree again, but they weren't there. Instead, something brown and white, whose small round head lolled grotesquely, hung over the branch.

Tom gasped with horror and nearly bumped into Joseph who had suddenly stopped.

'Mrs Musyoki's Jack Russell,' he said.

'That's where the dikdik was,' said Tom. 'Where we saw the leopard.'

'It's bad,' said Joseph. 'If the leopard has started to eat dogs and cats, it will go on and on.'

Tom thought of Tiger and a shiver ran down his spine. His feeling of safety evaporated. Joseph was going on again, skipping lightly across the stream on the stepping stones. Tom followed.

Safety in numbers, he thought.

They were halfway across when they heard people talking on the opposite hillside. They froze.

'I don't believe you.' A man was saying in a harsh, jeering voice. 'You never saw anything like that. You were in some stupid fantasy again.'

'Honestly, Dad. I did see it. Clear as daylight.'

Tom grabbed hold of Joseph, who was balancing on a small stone. He wobbled, and nearly toppled over into the water. Just in time, he clutched at Tom's arm and righted himself.

'What are you . . .'

'Sh! I know him. It's Pieter Hoven from school,' hissed Tom. 'I don't want him to see us. Let's hide. Quick!'

He turned, hopped back to the edge of the stream and threw himself down behind a clump of thick bushes. He looked out warily, afraid that Joseph hadn't followed, but Joseph was right behind him, moving so silently that Tom hadn't heard him coming.

Pieter Hoven and his father came out into the glade and stood looking round.

'Who are they?' whispered Joseph.

'Pieter Hoven and his dad. He's in my class at school. His dad's my dad's boss.'

Joseph gently parted the twigs in front of his face and his eyes narrowed as he peered out.

'Mr Hoven, yes, I know him,' he whispered. 'He's a bad man. His cook's son was my friend,

Joab. Joab saw Mr Hoven one day beating his wife. Mrs Hoven was hurt bad. Mr Hoven knew Joab saw him. The next day, Joab's dad got fired.'

'Careful,' said Tom. 'They might hear us.'

Pieter and Mr Hoven were walking along beside the stream now. Tom watched Pieter with surprise. He looked smaller beside the bulk of his heavily built father, and his swagger was gone. He walked fearfully, a little ahead, looking back all the time.

'I did see it,' he was saying. 'It *was* a leopard. I know it was.'

Tom breathed in sharply, then clapped his hand over his mouth. He could feel Joseph stiffen beside him, and knew he was as alert as a hunted hare.

'Pah!' Mr Hoven spat noisily on the ground. 'Rubbish. I don't know why I let you drag me down all the way here. It's high time this waste-land was cleared. It's a perfect cover for crooks and criminals. They ought to get rid of these trees and put a decent drainage system in along here to stop all this flooding.'

Pieter was searching along the ground with his eyes. A low branch caught at his hair. He looked up, and saw the remains of the Jack Russell hanging from the tree ahead of him.

'Dad!' he called out triumphantly. 'See, there *is* a leopard. It's hung something up the tree.'

Mr Hoven came over and looked at the bundle of white fur.

'Well I'll be . . . That black dentist's dog,' he said and Tom could see a slow smile spreading across his face. 'I'd never have believed it. A cheeky leopard, right at my back door.' He turned suddenly on Pieter. 'Have you told anyone about this?'

'No, Dad, honestly. I only saw it myself for the first time a little while ago.'

'Where? Where was it?' Mr Hoven looked round. 'Up the tree?'

'No.' Pieter pointed towards the bushes where Tom and Joseph were hiding. They shrank closer together. 'Right over there.'

A thrill of fear ran down Tom's spine. Had they walked into the leopard's lair? Was it behind them now? He raised himself to a crouching position ready for flight. Joseph was already on his haunches, looking round, piercing the undergrowth with the skilled eyes of a tracker.

Mr Hoven was walking to the edge of the stream. He hesitated, reluctant to trust his weight to the stepping stones.

Tom's heart was hammering and his palms were slippery with sweat.

'It's not there now, Dad,' Pieter called after him, and Tom felt a shudder of relief. 'It was going away from me when I saw it, back down along the stream.'

'Where? Where did it go?'

Mr Hoven turned his head and followed Pieter's pointing finger.

'I didn't see exactly. I . . . decided to go home.'

'Scared, were you? Yeah, well, serves you right. You shouldn't have been down here in the first place.' His mind was clearly only half on Pieter. He was looking round, assessing the glade, the trees, the stream.

'Anybody come down here?' he said suddenly. 'You ever see anyone down here?'

'I don't know, Dad,' said Pieter virtuously. 'I never, hardly ever, come down here myself.'

Mr Hoven wasn't listening to him.

'If I could get a decent view of it, I bet I could bring it down,' he said, talking to himself. 'The new rifle would do it. And it's quiet here. No interfering animal lovers to go telling tales.'

Pieter looked up at him, half-excited, half-appalled.

'You're not going to shoot it, are you, Dad?'

'Course I'm going to shoot it.' Mr Hoven slapped his meaty hands together. 'Think I want a leopard running wild round my house? I'll come down tomorrow, about half past five, when the light's beginning to go. Should be out on the prowl by then. Make sure you're ready. You keep me hanging around and you'll know all about it.'

Pieter gulped.

'You mean you want me to come with you?'

Mr Hoven turned on him.

'Of course I do. You need two pairs of eyes in this game. Now, you breathe a word of this to anybody and I'll have you for breakfast. You could get me into big trouble with those nancy boy conservationists at the KWS.'

'No, I wouldn't. I wouldn't say anything,' said Pieter, stepping backwards.

In the bushes, Tom felt something crawling up his leg. He looked down. A giant ant, more than a centimetre long, was running up his calf at incredible speed. He flicked it off with his finger and thumb and lost his balance. He grabbed hold of a branch of the bush to stop himself falling sideways into full view of the Hovens. The rustle of the leaves was shockingly loud. Tom righted himself, shut his eyes and buried his head in his knees. He was shaking.

'What was that? Up there?'

Mr Hoven had lifted his head and was staring straight at the bush.

'Nothing, Dad,' said Pieter, eager to get an answer. 'There's warthogs here. I saw their tracks. And there was a bird, with a long black tail. Really beautiful, it was.'

Mr Hoven frowned down at him.

'Birds with pretty tails? What are you going on about? It's time you learned to hunt. Do a man's job for a change. But don't you go telling your mother, or I'll . . .'

'I wouldn't. I never would.' Pieter was grinning

now, strutting along beside his father, copying the way Mr Hoven walked.

'She knows you come down here?' Mr Hoven had turned away from the stream and was starting up the hill. 'Come to think of it, what were you doing here in the first place? Are you up to something?'

Pieter's smile was wiped off his face.

'Nothing,' he said, and the whining note was back in his voice. 'There's a new boy in our class. He lives round here somewhere. I wanted to . . .'

'The Wilkinson kid?' Mr Hoven snorted. 'His old man's my new deputy manager. I don't give him six months. Boring nerd. Got no bite to him at all. What's the son like? Pathetic little creep too, is he?'

'Yeah,' said Pieter eagerly. 'He's really wet, Dad. He doesn't know anything.'

'Giving him the runaround, are you?' Mr Hoven clapped his son on the shoulder. 'That's right. You show him who's boss.'

Their voices faded as they disappeared into the trees.

Tom jumped to his feet, his face red with fury.

'Pathetic little creep, right? And my dad's a boring nerd?'

Joseph shook his shoulder.

'Didn't you hear, Tom? They're going to shoot the leopard!'

'Oh no they're not,' said Tom. 'Mr bully Hoven and his pathetic little creep of a son aren't going to shoot anything. Not unless they shoot me first.'

11

PLANS IN THE BOMA

Afra was climbing through the hole in the fence just as Joseph and Tom reached it. 'Did you see him?' she said. 'Is he still there?' Then she saw Tom's furious face. 'He's not – they haven't shot him already, have they?'

'No,' said Joseph, 'but we must do something quickly. That man, Mr Hoven, the one who fired Joab Opiyo's father, he was down there with his son.'

'With Pieter?' said Afra. 'Why?'

'Pieter had seen the leopard.'

'*What?*'

'He was on his way to find my garden,' said Tom, his voice shaking with anger. 'Says I'm a pathetic little creep and my dad's a boring nerd.'

'People like that say such things,' said Joseph. 'Didn't you hear him? He called Dr Musyoki "that black dentist". They are rubbish people. It is not worth it for you to think about their bad words.'

'I suppose so.' Tom felt the rage ebb a little from his head. 'I'd forgotten he'd said that about Dr Musyoki. You're right. They're just a load of creeps.'

'And you're saying that Pieter's seen our leopard?' demanded Afra. 'Is that why he took his dad down there? To show it to him?'

'Yes,' said Tom. 'We didn't see him ourselves, but we know he's still there. He's killed the Musyokis' Jack Russell. We saw it up the tree. Mr Hoven's planning to shoot the leopard tomorrow night. We've got to do something!'

Afra was pacing up and down. Stumpy, who had finished noisily slurping up the mush from his bowl, gave it a final push with his beak, came up to her and lovingly nibbled at her shoe. Over her shoulder, Joseph caught sight of a flash of yellow cloth.

'There's Mama,' he said in a low voice. 'We must go and talk somewhere else, or she will call us for something.'

'Not too near the house, then,' said Afra.

'Not close to our quarters either,' said Joseph.

Their eyes met.

'The *boma!*' they said together.

'What's that?' asked Tom.

'It's our den, our old fort, where we used to play when we were kids.' Afra was looking slightly embarrassed. 'We don't go there much now.'

Joseph was already slipping quietly away through the trees to the opposite corner of the garden.

'This garden's huge,' said Tom, following Afra and Stumpy. 'It's much bigger than ours.'

'Not really,' said Afra. 'I guess it seems bigger because it's all overgrown. Look, here's the fence. The boma's right here, under this tree.'

Joseph led the way to a tall tree whose lower branches dipped right down until they touched the ground. He parted some of them and went inside. The others followed him into an open space, enclosed on all sides by branches, which formed a perfect rounded roof. Some crumbling logs and a piece of old chewed plastic lay on the ground.

'My old ball!' said Afra, picking it up. 'How did it get like this, all squashed up and flat?'

'Porcupines, maybe,' said Joseph, looking round. 'This is a nice place, Afra. Why don't we come here any more?'

'It's brilliant,' said Tom, looking round enviously. 'It's the best base I've ever seen.'

Afra checked a log for creepy-crawlies and sat down on it. The others followed suit.

'I suppose we could try Uncle Titus again,' she said doubtfully.

'What's the point?' said Tom. 'Now that the leopard's eaten the Jack Russell, he'll say it's getting into the habit of hunting pets and he'll think it ought to be shot too.'

'But we could persuade him, *beg* him, to try something,' said Afra.

Joseph had been stirring the soft dust with the toe of his shoe. He looked up.

'You can't persuade Uncle Titus of anything, once he's made up his mind,' he said. 'But listen. I think that I have the answer. When I was a little boy, one day I was staying in our village with my grandfather—'

'What is this, Joseph?' interrupted Afra impatiently. 'Your life history? We've got a crisis on our hands here.'

'He was a great hunter when he was a young man,' went on Joseph, ignoring her. 'Just with his spear, he used to . . .'

'You're not suggesting we should *spear* the leopard, are you?' said Afra, scandalized.

'Tom,' said Joseph. 'Tie something around this girl's mouth until she lets me speak.'

Tom chuckled.

'Don't worry,' he said. 'I'll sit on her if she makes another squeak. Go on, Joseph.'

'Sometimes big animals come to the village, lions, leopard, elephants even. They break through the thorn fence and steal the cattle.'

'What . . .' began Afra.

Both boys pretended they were about to get to their feet.

'OK, OK,' she said, subsiding.

'They try to hunt the animal, but sometimes, if it's a leopard, it's too cunning. They can never see him. He hunts by night, so quietly, and steals his prey right under your nose. There is only one thing they can do.'

Afra and Tom were both gripped now, hanging on Joseph's words.

'They get all their drums and sticks and every noisy thing,' Joseph went on. 'They leave a lookout person for the leopard, then they light the sticks and wave them and make a big noise, very suddenly, just when the leopard thinks he is safe to steal a cow. The leopard gets very frightened and he runs away.'

'Yes,' breathed Afra. 'That's it, Joseph. You got it. We'll frighten him away!'

Tom was frowning, his mind already racing ahead, planning out the details.

'I've got my grandad's old football rattle,' he said. 'It's practically an antique but it makes enough noise to wake the dead, Mum thinks. What else can we use? Saucepan lids, whistles – could we get hold of a drum, do you think?'

Joseph nodded.

'A drum? No problem. I have a very good one. Very loud.'

'And I have an old kind of bugle thing,' said Afra. 'It's all messed up. You can't play music on it, but boy, does it squeal when you blow real hard!'

'Tomorrow evening, that's what Mr Hoven said,' Tom went on. 'About half past five. We'll have to act fast, before they arrive. Any time in the morning or afternoon would do. We'll have to track down the leopard first, then scare him away. It shouldn't be too difficult, as long as we can find him.'

He wanted to ask if the others thought it would be dangerous, if a frightened leopard might not turn and attack them, but Afra was already speaking.

'We'll find him all right,' said Afra. 'He probably doesn't go too far from where he's stashed his kill.'

'Then we'll rush him, and make a terrible noise, and he'll get so scared he'll run off,' said Tom triumphantly.

Joseph shook his head.

'But if he is up a tree already, he will just climb higher. We cannot get him down from there. We have to wait until he comes down by himself. Then he will run away.'

'But that's just when the Hovens will be after him!' said Tom. 'What if they shoot him before we manage to make him run away?'

'We'll have to do it tonight. Now!' Afra jumped to her feet.

'It's too late,' said Joseph. 'Look, it's already nearly dark. We'll never find him now. And it's too dangerous for us to hunt him in the dark.'

He was right. The sudden African night had all but fallen. There was only the faintest glow of light around them now and, almost as they looked, the green of the leaves was leaching away to a dark, indistinguishable grey.

'Oh no, it's late! I must go!' said Tom. 'Mum'll phone Lise Hoven in a minute. I told her I was going round to Pieter's house to borrow an atlas.'

'What?' said Afra incredulously. 'She doesn't mind you being friends with that jerk but she doesn't want you to hang out with us?'

Tom looked uneasy.

'Mr Hoven is Dad's boss,' he said.

'Your poor dad,' said Afra.

'Yeah, I suppose,' said Tom. 'Look, I must go.'

'But we didn't finish planning,' said Afra, 'and it's Saturday tomorrow, so we won't see each other at school. We have to decide what time we're going to meet.'

'I'll put a note in the fence as soon as I know when I can get away,' said Tom. He peered out through the screen of leaves. 'Hey, how do I get out of this place? It's like a jungle out there.'

Afra scooped Stumpy up in her arms.

'Time you were safely tucked up in your night cage, big gosling,' she said, and she led the way out of the boma towards the bungalow.

Tom stopped suddenly when they reached the verandah.

'Hey, I nearly forgot,' he said. 'Lend me your atlas, Afra. It's my alibi.'

*

Debbie was lifting the receiver on the telephone when he ran in through the front door.

'There you are at last,' she said, putting it back on the cradle again. 'I was getting worried. You mustn't stay out after dark, Tom. It's not safe. I was just about to phone Lise Hoven.'

'Sorry, Mum.' Tom sounded as casual as he could, though his heart had lurched at the trouble he had just averted. 'It took me ages to find Pieter. Mrs Hoven was out and I couldn't get him to hear me.'

'What's their house like?' said Debbie curiously.

'Oh, you know,' said Tom, wishing for once that Bella would appear. 'It's quite big. You know.'

He opened the atlas ostentatiously and pretended to study it.

'No, I don't know.' Debbie wasn't going to be put off. 'Is it much bigger than ours?'

'I didn't notice,' said Tom. 'What's for supper?'

Debbie sighed and gave up.

'It was going to be lasagne,' she said, 'but I spent the whole afternoon putting up curtains and I ran out of time. I'll get some hamburgers out of the freezer and we can open a tin of beans.'

Simon opened the door and came in.

'How did it go today?' said Debbie, eyeing him anxiously.

'Not good.' Simon slammed his briefcase down on the table by the phone. 'I don't know what's the matter with the man. I can't seem to do anything right. Thank God he left the office early today. He's lazy, as well as everything else. Apparently he bunks off work quite often. It's the only thing that's going to keep me sane.'

Debbie picked up his briefcase and put it down tidily on a chair.

'Simon, you've got to find a way of getting on with him, you know you have.'

He dropped a kiss on her cheek.

'I know, love. Don't worry. It'll be OK.'

Supper was a silent meal that evening. Tom ate wordlessly, worrying about the next day, only half aware of his father's quiet depression and Debbie's obvious anxiety. Not even Bella was there to liven things up. She was in bed already.

As he ate, Tom's mind was going over and over the plan to scare the leopard, aware that something was missing. Suddenly, as he was putting a forkful of beans to his mouth, he realized what it was. The fork froze in mid-air.

What would happen tomorrow if he came face to face with Pieter, while he and the others were trying to scare the leopard away? If Pieter recognized him, he'd tell Mr Hoven who he was, and Mr Hoven would be furious. He'd look around for someone to punish, and who would that someone be? His new export manager, Simon Wilkinson. Dad might even get the sack. And if he did, the whole family would be back on the plane to England before they'd been in Africa for as much as a week.

Tom put the forkful of beans into his mouth and went on thinking. A couple of days ago, he'd have loved the idea of going home, and seeing Scott, and being back in his old school. But now he didn't feel so sure. If he left now, he'd never get to know Afra and Joseph properly, or have the chance to hold Kiksy, or find out what happened to the leopard. He'd never get to go on safari in a game park, and see the elephants and rhinos like they were in films. And then it would be awful, too, for Dad. He might not get another job easily, and if he was unemployed he'd be miserable, and when he was miserable he quarrelled with Mum, and that was the worst of all.

'What's the matter with you, Tom?' said Simon.

'Nothing,' said Tom. 'Why is Mr Hoven so horrible to you, Dad?'

'Search me,' said Simon. Supper, a glass of beer and the prospect of the weekend ahead seemed to be cheering him up. 'He's just a natural bully, I suppose.'

'You've got to stand up to bullies,' said Tom seriously. 'If you let them push you around, you're finished. And you've got to let them know right away, before they start thinking you're a softy, or a nerd, or anything.'

'Yes, well . . .' Simon began dismissively. Then

he stopped and looked at Tom. 'Thanks,' he said. 'I'll think about that.'

He swallowed another mouthful of beer.

Tom's mind took off and began leaping along a trail of its own. It jumped from the idea of bullies, to the idea of thugs, and from the thought of thugs to an actual picture of bank robbers. He imagined them, just like he'd seen them in a crime film once, disguised with stockings over their faces. The effect had been horrible. Really scary. The men hadn't even looked like people, never mind individuals with recognizable faces.

He pushed his chair back from the table.

'Got some homework to do,' he said. 'I'm off upstairs.'

12

TERROR IN THE NIGHT

Tom had only been in his parents' bedroom a couple of times so far. He opened the door and went in on tiptoe. He didn't want to put the light on in case one of them came up the stairs suddenly and caught him, but without it the dark would have been impenetrable.

There were fitted cupboards with long white-painted doors down one side of the room. He went round the bed and opened the first door. In the cupboard behind was a rack of hangers with his dad's suits and trousers hanging up. Behind the next door was a stack of drawers. He wrenched open the top one.

'Dad's stuff,' he muttered.

He tried the next door and knew at once, by the scent of cosmetics, that the drawers behind it held Debbie's things. He was lucky this time. He opened the top drawer and found some tights, quite a few pairs, neatly rolled up.

I'll have to cut them up, he thought, and she's bound to miss them.

He sorted through them quickly, hoping to find some that had already been holed, that she wouldn't be so likely to miss, but then he heard the sound of the kitchen door opening downstairs. He stuffed two pairs of black tights in his pocket and ran over to the door. Before he got to it, it opened.

Bella stood there, her eyes puffy with sleep, her pink nightie trailing on the floor.

'When's it coming?' she said. 'That thing?'

She looked so worried that Tom felt sorry for her. He bent down and picked her up. She nestled her head into his shoulder, and he knew her thumb had crept into her mouth. She felt good, lying there, and he thought suddenly of Kiksy's arms encircling Afra's neck.

'It's not going to come,' he said. 'It's going away tomorrow. I'll make sure it doesn't get you.'

She was half asleep again already. He took her back into her little bedroom, settled her in her bed, and tiptoed out.

He went to bed himself soon after, but he didn't sleep. He was aware as never before of the noises of the night. He heard his parents move about downstairs, opening and shutting the kitchen door. A little later, he heard the hinge of his bedroom door squeak, and the patter of clawed paws on the woodblock floor that fringed the rug as Tiger trotted into the room and leaped lightly onto the bed to settle into her usual sleeping place by his feet.

Outside he could hear, alongside the rumble of

traffic and the occasional blast of a car horn, the noise of the African night. Crickets whirred, a night bird made a 'chucker chucker' call and a creature nearby squealed intermittently in anger or fear.

The pendulum clock in the hall downstairs chimed. Tom had lost count of the hours but soon after it had struck, he heard the stairs creak as his parents came up to bed. For a while the sound of running water came from the bathroom, and he could hear the murmur of their voices from their bedroom. Then they were quiet. At last he was feeling drowsy. He let his mind freewheel, on the edge of sleep.

The sound that roused him was so eerie it raised the hairs on his neck and made him sit bolt upright in bed. It was a rasping, grunting sound, short and throaty, like the rusty blade of a saw on unyielding wood. For a moment he thought he'd imagined it, and was about to lie down when he heard it again.

Only one creature could be making such a noise. It had to be the leopard.

The leopard grunted again, four times, its voice sounding out in the still night air in a strange, sinister monotone. Then it fell silent.

Tom shivered.

I bet Afra and Joseph heard him, he thought. I bet loads of people did. He's given himself away properly now.

He wondered if leopards ever came into houses and snatched people from their beds. Joseph had said that thorn fences didn't keep them out. Maybe walls wouldn't either. In the glow of moonlight coming through the round window above his bed, he could see that his bedroom door had swung half open. He'd feel safer with it shut.

He got out of bed and nearly tripped on the rug. He put his hand down on the end of the bed to steady himself and made a discovery. Tiger wasn't there.

A cold hand seemed to close round Tom's throat, making it hard for him to breathe. He stood stock-still for a moment, not knowing what to do, then made a dash for the stairs and tore down them three at a time, nearly falling headlong in his rush. He ran into the sitting room, put the light on, and stood there for a moment, blinded, blinking through half-shut eyes at the empty sofa and armchairs.

'Tiger!' he said softly. 'Tiger, come here!'

But he could tell by a kind of stillness in the room that it was empty. He ran through the hall and opened the kitchen door. His eyes were adapting to the harsh electric light now and he could see at a glance that Tiger wasn't there. Fruitlessly, he looked into the little dining room, that was still full of unopened packing cases. Tiger wasn't anywhere down here, on the ground floor.

He raced silently up the stairs again and stood hesitating outside his parents' door. It was closed.

Tiger can't have opened it and gone in there and shut it again, he thought.

He looked round. Bella's door was ajar. He tiptoed into her room.

'Tiger,' he whispered. 'Please be here. Tiger, come on. It's me.'

Nothing stirred in the darkness.

Maybe I was wrong, he thought. Maybe she's still in my room after all.

Back in his room, he put the light on and looked everywhere, even under the bed and in the wardrobe, knowing it was hopeless.

She can't have gone out into the garden, he thought. She *mustn't* be out there.

He turned off his light and pulled the curtains back from the main window.

He saw the little black cat at once. She was crouching in a pool of moonlight on the lawn, tense, as if ready to spring, looking intently ahead. Tom had watched her doing that hundreds of times before. She must have seen some little creature, a beetle or a toad and, cat-like, she was stalking it.

Without stopping to think, he ran downstairs again and dashed through the sitting room to the verandah doors. Dad had locked and bolted them before he'd gone up to bed, but the bolts were oiled and the locks new. It was easy to undo them.

Tom opened the door and stepped out onto the verandah.

His heart was thumping painfully in his chest. He'd never been outside so late at night before.

Nothing's different – it's only the garden, he told himself, but a consuming fear was touching him, something as ancient as man, a terror of the dark and its dangers, of teeth and claws and a swift, fearless enemy.

He hesitated. The verandah, surrounded by man-made walls and roofed with man-sawn timbers, felt somehow safe, but the lawn was no-man's land. He'd be easy meat out there.

Why am I making such a big deal out of this? he thought. The leopard's probably miles away.

Tiger, intent on her prey, hadn't turned her head. She looked so innocent, so homely and tame, playing at being a hunter, that Tom couldn't imagine that any harm could come to her. But as he watched, he saw in his mind's eye Bella in Tiger's place, Bella playing there on the lawn, absorbed in a toy, a frown of concentration on her baby face, oblivious to anything outside her safe, secure world. Tiger was just as clueless as Bella would be, faced with the cunning and hunger of a leopard.

He took a deep breath, stepped off the verandah and ran towards the cat. Then he heard it, a deep, throaty cough, a warning, a threat, and he turned round and saw the leopard.

He was crouching in the shade of a tree and Tom could see only half of him, only the outline of one side of his head, one round ear, one spotted cheek and one stern, unwinking eye that seemed to frown at him from under a heavy brow.

He was no more than three metres away, and was tensed, ready to spring. If Tom had hesitated a moment longer, Tiger's neck would have been snapped in two by one bite of those massive jaws.

Tiger had heard the snarl. With a terrified yowl she streaked past Tom, up the verandah steps and into the house. Tom was facing the leopard alone.

Terror froze him for a long moment, but then his brain cleared and he felt alert, every muscle alive and ready for action. The leopard was still crouching, watching him, assessing him. Then he bent his head lower to the ground, curled the soft furry flesh over his lips away from his dagger-like canines and grunted again, and the moonlight glinted on his long whiskers and the white fur of his neck, deceptively soft fur, as silky as Tiger's.

Instinctively, Tom drew his own lips back, showing his teeth. His brain, working at full speed, instructed him not to run. The leopard would be upon him instantly. He had to stand his ground.

He shifted his position on the grass, bracing himself for whatever might come, and one bare foot knocked against a stone. Holding the leopard's eyes with his, he bent his knees and felt for it with his hand.

Although the leopard had barely moved, Tom sensed a tightening in his powerful haunches, as though he was gathering himself for a spring. Tom righted himself, the stone in his hand, and flung it with all his might towards the leopard's head.

The moment it left his hand, terror seized him again. Even before the stone bounced harmlessly off the trunk of the tree behind the leopard's head, the huge animal was on his feet, a rumbling growl bubbling in his throat, and for a couple of seconds, which seemed to last as long as an hour, Tom was convinced that he would spring. He put his hands up in a futile attempt to protect his face.

'Go away! You've got to go,' he cried hoarsely. 'You can't stay here! Leave me alone!'

Then, to his incredulous relief, he saw that the leopard was turning, moving its muscular body out of the shade of the tree, loping away with easy grace across the grass towards the gap in the fence at the bottom of the garden.

For a moment or two, Tom watched as he crossed the moonlit lawn, then he was hidden by the bushes, his spots a perfect camouflage in the darkness, and only the white tip of his curled tail showed as he disappeared into the night.

As if he'd been released from a spell, Tom took off, sprinting back to the verandah. He burst into the sitting room, locked the doors behind him and stood with his back to them, unable to move. He was shaking from head to foot and his knees felt as weak as water. His heart was thudding violently. He could feel its pulse hammering in his ears.

Then he heard a pathetic mewing and looking down, he saw Tiger, hunched up and shivering under the coffee table.

'Oh Tiger,' he said, 'he nearly got you. You nearly got eaten,' and he scrabbled under the table, pulled the little cat out and held her tightly in his arms. He felt a sob rise in his throat and tears run down his cheeks.

'Don't ever do that to me again,' he said, rubbing his wet face on her fur. 'Don't ever go out at night again.'

He realized that he had no idea how she had escaped from the house in the first place. The thought that a window or door might still be open, that Tiger might get out again, or even that the leopard might be able to get in, made his stomach tighten with dread.

Now that the verandah doors were shut and locked, the sitting room at least was secure. Cautiously, he did the rounds of the ground floor again, jumpily aware of every shadowy corner and the creak of every floorboard. All the doors and windows were shut. There was no way in or out down here.

Still holding Tiger, who was lying with her

forepaws on his shoulder, her anxious claws digging almost painfully into his skin, he went back up to his room. The curtain was billowing out in the night breeze. It was his own window that had been open.

He looked down from it and noticed for the first time that the corner of the verandah roof stood out from the wall a couple of metres below his sill. Tiger must have gone down that way. It would have been an easy jump for her, and another easy leap down to the ground. He shuddered. Leopards could climb, he knew that. It might have been an easy jump for the leopard up to his bedroom window too.

He shut the window with a snap and, just to be on the safe side, pulled his chair over to the door and wedged it underneath the handle. If the leopard, by some incredible cunning, managed to defeat all the locks and bars and find its way into the house and up the stairs, at least he'd have a bit of warning when it pushed against his door.

But he didn't want to think of that. He didn't want to imagine all that terror in his room.

He climbed back into bed, felt the familiar weight of Tiger on his feet, and fell asleep.

13

TOM GIVES EVERYONE
THE SLIP

Tom slept late the following morning. He rolled over at last, yawned and opened his eyes. Bright sunshine was bathing his bedroom with a hard white light. He lay still for a while, enjoying the comfort of his bed, then realized that he was too hot, and that the room was stuffy and airless. He sat up and leaned over to open the window, and the memory of last night came rushing back.

He looked round for Tiger. She wasn't on the bed, but when he called she came out, stretching herself, from under it and stood against his legs, waiting to be picked up. He could tell she was still terrified. She looked round nervously from the vantage point of his arms, and didn't try to lick his face, or purr, as she usually did.

Tom put her down and reached for the pile of clothes lying in a jumble on the floor. Then he caught sight of the clock on his bedside table.

Half past eleven! He couldn't believe it. He'd slept for hours and hours.

He dragged his clothes on, pulled the chair away from the door and ran downstairs. Debbie was in the kitchen, looking out of the window. She turned round as Tom came in.

'Hello, love. I thought you'd never wake up,' she said.

She'd left his breakfast things out on the table. Tom sat down and poured some cereal into his bowl. He wanted to tell her about last night, but he knew he couldn't. She'd panic completely, and within minutes the place would be full of marksmen, hunting the leopard down. In spite of the terror of his desperate encounter in the moonlight, he didn't want the leopard to be destroyed like vermin, to be a hunted creature, to know that its magnificent power had been humiliatingly brought down, and that its warm fur had become stiff and lifeless, matted with blood.

In fact, he was beginning to think he must have imagined the whole thing, the strangeness and wildness and danger of it. His confrontation with the leopard seemed fantastic, in this ordinary kitchen, with Mum sorting out the laundry, and Bella singing a tuneless song in the hall outside. Everything was shatteringly normal.

Then he saw a man just outside the kitchen window. He was wearing blue overalls and his dark skin showed through the sparse white hairs on his balding scalp.

'Hey, there's someone in the garden!' he said.

'It's Timothy, our new gardener,' said Debbie, a little grandly. 'He's bringing his niece along to see me this afternoon. She might help me in the house.'

Timothy's head disappeared from sight as he bent down over a flowerbed.

What if the leopard left his paw prints around the place? thought Tom. I'd better get out there quick and look round and cover them up.

He tried to eat faster, slurping the mushy cereal and milk up with his spoon, then gave up, lifted the bowl to his lips and drank the rest of it down, letting the sugar at the bottom of the bowl drain into his mouth.

'Don't do that,' said Debbie sharply. 'It's disgusting.'

'Sorry,' said Tom, putting the bowl down and wiping his mouth with the back of his hand.

He pushed his chair back and stood up.

'Where are you off to?' Debbie was looking at him suspiciously. 'Don't go off and disappear again. Lise Hoven phoned this morning. She's invited me to come to her club.'

Tom's heart sank. Mum seemed to be getting really friendly with Mrs Hoven. It was only a matter of time before that whole business of the atlas came out. He'd really be in trouble then.

'Apparently there's a wonderful pool and some tennis courts,' Debbie went on. 'You'd like it, I know you would. You might meet some boys of your own age.'

'I can't go out this morning, Mum,' said Tom. 'Got too much homework.'

'But you were doing homework all yesterday evening.' Approval and disapproval were balanced equally in Debbie's voice.

'Got a lot to catch up on,' said Tom.

'Well, you can finish it all while I'm out and give me a hand this afternoon. I want to get the place straight. The Hovens are coming round for a drink this evening.'

'*What?*' said Tom.

Simon came into the kitchen.

'What was that you said, Debs?' he said.

Debbie looked at him defiantly.

'I was talking to Lise on the phone. She's been very kind and friendly, taking me round and showing me where to go and that. She's such a nice, quiet person. I think she's a bit lonely. And Tom's made friends with Pieter, so I thought . . .'

'I don't care what you thought.' Simon slapped the armful of files he'd been holding down on the table. 'I have to spend all day in the office with that man. I'm damned if I want him in my house at the weekend.'

'I'm sorry,' said Debbie, aggrieved. 'I was only acting for the best. I thought . . .'

'I know what you thought. You thought if I have "a nice quiet drink" and "a little chat" with Rudi Hoven, he and I would suddenly become bosom buddies and all our troubles would be solved. I don't want you meddling in things at the office Debbie. I won't have it.'

They glared at each other. Simon marched to the door.

'I'm going to call them and tell them Bella's gone down with measles or the cat's been run over or something.'

'Simon!' cried Debbie. 'You can't! It would be so rude.'

Simon stopped.

'No,' he said. 'I can't. I'll have to go through with it. Thanks for ruining my weekend.'

Tom had been standing stock-still by the fridge while the implications sank in. He hated the idea of the Hovens setting foot in this house, of that red-faced bully humiliating Dad, and his loathsome son looking round, gathering ammunition so he could tease Tom more effectively at school.

And what about the leopard? If the Hovens had agreed to come round this evening, it meant that Mr Hoven was likely to go out hunting earlier than he'd said.

He had to have an urgent meeting with Joseph and Afra. They had to decide what to do.

'When are you going out, Mum?' he said, as casually as he could. 'Will you be back for lunch?'

She looked harassed.

'No. You'll have to make yourself a sandwich. Anyway, you've only just had breakfast. I haven't got time to worry about that now. Lise'll be here any minute. I wish you'd come with us, Tom. I know you'd like it at the club.'

'Tom's coming with me, into town,' interrupted Simon. 'I'm sure he'd prefer that. I've got to do a few bits and pieces, then we can go and eat somewhere.'

'I'm sorry, Dad,' said Tom, making his expression as regretful as he could. 'I've got to finish my homework. Honestly.'

'You can't stay here on your own,' said Debbie. 'Anything might happen.'

Tom caught sight of Timothy's head as he straightened his back from his weeding.

'The gardener's here,' he said. 'Anyway, I'm not exactly five years old any more.'

The doorbell rang.

'That's Lise now,' said Debbie, walking past Simon, not meeting his eye.

Tom sidled out of the kitchen and ran up the stairs. He'd only have to wait a few minutes and the coast would be clear. He rummaged around in the bottom of his wardrobe, where he'd dumped a whole load of stuff, and pulled out his grandad's old football rattle. Then he put on a brown sweater, the best camouflage he could find, stuffed Debbie's tights into his pocket and went out into the corridor.

Debbie and Mrs Hoven had gone into the sitting room, and he could hear Dad starting the car at the front of the house.

He was about to run downstairs when he had an idea. He ripped a piece of paper out of one of his exercise books and wrote 'Do not disturb' on it, in thick black felt tip. Then he turned on his radio, pressed the tuning buttons till he found some music, and left it playing. He went out and shut the door, tore a hole in his notice and hung it over the doorknob. It might just keep his parents at bay if they came home too soon.

He went down to the kitchen, let himself out through the back door and circled to the right, round the side of the house, to avoid the gardener. Mum and Mrs Hoven were still in the sitting room. He could hear their voices coming out through the verandah doors. He waited impatiently while Mum finished putting on Bella's shoes, and listened as they went slowly out through the front door. At last, he heard the doors of Mrs Hoven's car slam, and the engine start.

He looked round the side of the house to the back. Timothy must still be working under the kitchen window, out of sight, on the far side. Tom ran up the verandah steps and looked into the sitting room, wanting to check up on Tiger. She was under the coffee table, where she'd taken refuge last night, sitting on her haunches, still clearly traumatized by her encounter with the leopard.

'He won't come back,' said Tom reassuringly. 'He's going away today, I promise you,' but he knew that it would be a long time before Tiger set foot in the garden again.

Keeping his ears cocked for Timothy's footsteps, Tom went back to the edge of the lawn and looked under the bushes where the leopard had lain in wait last night. The ground was quite hard, and he couldn't see much sign that a big animal had been there, but he guessed that Timothy's tracking skills would be better than his, so he scuffed the ground over, just in case.

He was tired of all this secrecy, tired of having to hide all the time, and keep secrets, and tell lies. He made his mind up suddenly.

If we manage to scare the leopard away I'm going to tell them everything tonight, he thought. I'll tell them about the atlas, and that Joseph and Afra are my friends, and I'll them they can't stop me, I'm going round next door whenever I want to and I'm going to see my mates whatever they say.

Then he ran down the garden, squeezed through the gap in the fence and began to work his way through the undergrowth to the hole in the chain link at the back of the Toveys' garden.

14

A PERFECT HIDING PLACE

Afra was practically dancing with impatience when Tom burst out of the bushes onto the lawn, where she and Joseph were in the process of tying a fourth piece of clothing to the tree.

'Where *were* you?' she said. 'We've been waiting for you all morning. We went to check for messages by the fence fifty times at least. Look, this is the fourth scarf we've wrapped round this tree, only we've run out of scarves and it's my old sweater.'

Tom grinned shamefacedly.

'I'm sorry, I didn't look out of my window,' he said. 'But I came as soon as I could.'

'You didn't *look?*' said Joseph indignantly. 'What have you been doing all this morning?'

'I . . . Well, if you want to know the truth, I was asleep,' said Tom. 'I was up half the night. You're not going to believe this. I saw him. Right up close. I thought he was going to get me.'

'You saw the *leopard?*' said Afra.

'Yes,' said Tom, launching into the story of what had happened.

'You threw a stone at a leopard?' said Joseph

when he'd told them everything. 'While it was hunting? Man, you're crazy. I cannot believe that you are still alive.'

'Wow,' said Afra, shaking her head. 'You must have been pretty scared, but I feel kind of envious. It must have been amazing.'

'It was,' said Tom with a shudder. 'But listen, we've got to move earlier than we thought. My mum's gone and invited the Hovens round for a drink this evening.'

'Those people? Why on earth?' said Afra. 'They're so horrible, they're . . . Wait a minute! This means that they'll be busy right when they were planning to go hunting.'

'Yes,' said Joseph. 'And I think that Mr Hoven will go after the leopard earlier. Perhaps they're down there already. Now, maybe!'

'Exactly,' said Tom. 'We must go right away. Have you got your things to make a noise with? Look, here's my grandad's rattle. It's brilliant. It'll scare everything for miles around.'

'Our stuff's all ready,' said Afra. 'We've got the drum and the saucepan lids, but I can't find the trumpet anywhere. I'll go get the bag.'

'Bring some scissors with you!' Tom called after her.

'Scissors? Why?'

'For our disguise,' he said. 'You'll see.'

She was back a moment later with a bag in her hand and Kiksy clinging to her shoulder.

'Why did you wake Kiksy?' said Joseph disapprovingly. 'You can't take a bushbaby with you when you're hunting a leopard.'

'I didn't wake him,' said Afra, detaching one of the bushbaby's sticky little hands from her ear. 'He was awake already. He wants a bit of company, that's all.' She set Kiksy gently down on the ground. 'Go back to your nest,' she said. 'Go back to sleep. It's still your bedtime.'

The little creature stared back at her out of his enormous, unwinking eyes.

'Something's unsettling him,' said Afra. 'He's scared. He usually sleeps right up until it's dark.'

'Maybe he saw the leopard last night too,' said Tom. 'Maybe he came into your garden after he left ours.'

'Leave him,' said Joseph impatiently. 'Did you bring my drum?'

'Yes, and a few other things,' said Afra, handing a pair of scissors to Tom. 'What did you want these for? I don't get it.'

Tom took Debbie's tights out of his pocket and scissored the legs apart. Then he pulled one over his face. Joseph and Afra stepped back in horror.

'That's very good, Tom,' said Joseph delightedly. 'It's a very good disguise. Even your own mother would not recognize you now.'

'I hope she wouldn't recognize her tights, either,' said Tom.

Afra was looking at him through narrowed eyes.

'She would know you, though,' she said. 'I can still tell it's you. We'll just have to muss it up a little.'

She went over to Stumpy's water bowl, tipped some water onto the ground and stirred some dust into it to make a little mud.

'Wait,' said Tom. 'Before you do that, I'm going to cut a couple of eye holes. I can't see very well.'

He took the tights off, snipped a couple of narrow slits in them and put the mask on again. Enthusiastically, Afra applied smears of mud to his cheeks and forehead.

'Excellent,' she said. 'Not even Tiger would know you now.'

Tom snipped holes in another leg of the tights and handed it to Afra. She took it gingerly.

'Can you breathe with this thing on?' she said. 'Isn't it dangerous?'

'Course you can breathe,' said Tom. 'It's not like a plastic bag or anything. Go ahead and try it.'

Grimacing, she took it, and slipped it over her head. Joseph did the same.

'Come on, Tom,' said Afra, sounding a little muffled behind the nylon mask. 'Do it to us too. We've got to get going.'

'Wait a minute,' said Tom, whose face was beginning to sweat under the nylon mesh. 'We can't wear these all afternoon. We'll die of heat.' He pushed his mask up till it made a kind of cap on his head. 'Phew, that's better! It'll be OK like this. We can pull them down really quickly when the Hovens come.'

A few minutes later, the three of them were through the Toveys' fence and in the forest beyond.

'We must go down to the stream first and try to find where the leopard is resting for the day,' said Joseph quietly. 'Then we must select a hiding place for ourselves. It's still early. Perhaps we'll have to wait for a long time. We must remain very quiet, without speaking.'

'No problem,' said Afra, nodding seriously.

The boys exchanged looks over her head.

'Give me a break, you two,' said Afra, grinning. 'I can keep my mouth shut same as anybody.'

Joseph led the way down the path. He walked silently, his feet seeming, with instinctive wisdom, to avoid any dead leaf that might rustle, or dead twig that might give them away with a snap. Tom tried to copy him, grateful to Joseph for going first. Here, in the forest, the leopard's own territory, some of last night's fear was returning, and his skin prickled as the hairs on it rose.

They reached the glade, but didn't emerge into the open. For a long moment, Joseph looked up and downstream. There was no sign of the Hovens. Tom felt in his bones that they were not there, and was not surprised when Joseph whispered, almost inaudibly, 'They have not come yet. We can search for the leopard now.'

The white fur of the little dog was no longer hanging in the tree. The remains of the carcass had dropped to the ground where some scavenger had been tearing at it, and had dragged it towards the stream.

Joseph's watchful eyes scanned the clearing, looking down at the ground for tracks and up into the trees for unusually dense patches of shadow.

'Come on,' he breathed to the other two, and on silent feet he began to work his way around the edge of the glade, keeping close enough to cover so that he could hide with a moment's warning.

Afra and Tom followed him, looking over their shoulders uneasily from time to time when a gust of wind rustled the leaves, or a bird took off with a noisy cry.

Joseph turned.

'I do not think he is nearby at the moment,' he said at last. 'Shall we go down or up the stream to look for him?'

Afra considered for a moment.

'We'd better wait here,' she whispered. 'We know the Hovens will come this way. Supposing they come while we're away, and the leopard comes back from a different direction? They'd get to him first.'

'Afra's right,' said Tom. 'We'll have to stay

here. If we don't see the leopard before the Hovens come, we'll have to track *them* till they find the leopard, and scare him off before Mr Hoven gets a shot at him.'

'OK,' said Joseph. 'I agree. So now we must find a hiding place. I know a good one. I waited there once when I was watching a bushbuck.'

He led the others out into the open and they followed him a little way upstream to a dense clump of bushes. They pushed their way in behind them and looked round.

It was a perfect hiding place. There was room for all three of them to sit comfortably on the ground. They had a good view of the glade on all sides, but were screened by the foliage at the same time.

'This is great,' said Afra, sitting down on the soft dusty ground. 'Like the boma, only smaller.'

'Shh,' said Joseph. 'Don't talk.'

Afra reached into her bag, fetched out the drum and the saucepan lids and set them out on the ground where they could be snatched up quickly.

She was still bending over when something small and furry landed with a thump on her back.

'Kiksy!' she gasped. 'Oh boy, you startled me.'

The bushbaby ran up her back and settled in his favourite place on her shoulder. He sat there trembling, looking round with nervous eyes.

'It's not good for him to be here,' muttered Joseph.

'Well, I can hardly take him back now, can I?' said Afra in a fierce whisper. 'We'll just have to make the best of it.'

It was mid-afternoon now, the hottest part of the day. Afra, Tom and Joseph settled themselves on the ground.

'We must stay still and quiet,' whispered Joseph. 'And wait.'

The minutes ticked by. Half an hour passed. Afra shifted herself round to a more comfortable position and put her back against a boulder. She slid down until she was half lying, with Kiksy curled up in a downy ball on her chest. For a while, she stared up into the trees overhead, watching the shifting patterns of light and shade as the leaves moved gently, responding to the smallest currents of air, then her eyelids closed and she slept.

Joseph, squatting on his haunches, was sleepy too. His head fell forward onto his knees and he jerked himself upright again.

Tom touched him on the shoulder.

'It's OK, you can sleep if you like,' he mouthed. 'I'll keep watch.'

Gratefully, Joseph lay down and a moment later his eyes were shut too.

Tom sat with his arms wrapped round his knees, looking out through the veil of leaves. He had no desire to sleep. There was unfinished business between him and the leopard. For some reason, which he would never know, the leopard had spared his life last night. He would try his best to save the leopard's life now.

He was alert to every tiny movement in the forest all around, alive to every sound. Once there came the cheerful crashing of leaves and branches overhead as a monkey, perhaps the same one who had woken him on his first morning in Africa, swung himself effortlessly through the trees above, oblivious to the humans hiding below.

A little later his eye was caught by something moving near his feet and he looked down to see a chongalulu, its hundreds of legs rippling effortlessly over the uneven ground.

Tom frowned at it. He had unfinished business with the Hovens, too. And with Mum and Dad, come to think of it. He wasn't looking forward to telling them everything this evening.

He was just trying to imagine exactly what Mr Hoven would do when he realized that three children were determined to scare the leopard away from him, when he heard a faint scratching noise over to the left. He turned his head and craned his neck, trying to see where the noise was coming from. Then his heart gave a sickening thump.

The leopard was pacing along the stream, the muscles in his heavy neck bunching as he walked, his golden eyes sweeping the glade. Stiff with fear and excitement, Tom turned to shake Joseph gently by the shoulder.

Joseph's eyes flew open, read the signal in Tom's and sat up. They looked at Afra. Tom asked a wordless question, Joseph answered it with a nod, waited while Tom moved his hand until it was ready to clamp down on Afra's mouth, then he bent down and whispered in Afra's ear, 'Afra, do not make a sound. The leopard is here.'

Afra was awake instantly, and, her first thought for Kiksy, felt for the bushbaby with her hands, but Kiksy had sensed the leopard's presence and with a hoot of fear had run up to the top of the bush. He sat there, tensed and ready to spring up into the tree above.

Tom saw the leopard move his powerful head, saw his eyes focus on the bushbaby, noting its position, watching where it went, as if he was marking it down for the moment after dark when he would be ready to hunt. Then his eyes fell again, and rested unblinkingly on the bush where Tom, Afra and Joseph were crouching, their muscles stiff with tension, watching him, braced for him to move.

The leopard's head turned away. He was looking across to the far side of the stream now. He had heard a twig snap. Somebody was coming down the path.

15

SAVED – FOR NOW

Tom hardly heard Afra's tiny gasp as Joseph's hand closed warningly over her arm. He was paralysed with fear, his old deep fear of the leopard, and a new fear, of being discovered by a furious Mr Hoven with a gun. He wanted desperately to stay where he was, to cling to the safety of this hiding place.

Afra, her face set, was pulling her stocking mask over her face. Joseph's was in place already. Tom fumbled for his, and pulled it down with trembling fingers. Wearing it made him feel momentarily better. It gave him a small flush of courage.

His eyes were raking the far side of the glade, watching the place where the sound of the snapped twig had come from. Out of the corner of his eye he was aware that the leopard was almost unnaturally still, only his nose twitching.

For a full half minute, which felt like half an hour, nothing moved. Then Tom saw it. A gleam of sunlight was catching on something shiny and metallic, which certainly hadn't been there a moment before, a long round tube protruding from behind a thick clump of bushes. Tom's brain took a moment to catch up with his eyes, and then he recognized it.

It was the barrel of a gun.

Before he had time to think of the consequences, he snatched up his rattle and lunged forward out of the hiding place, just as Mr Hoven, with Pieter close behind him, stepped cautiously out into the open, the leopard in his sights. He had a momentary glimpse of Mr Hoven with the gun raised to his shoulder, and of Pieter, standing taut with excitement beside him, then he raced towards the leopard, spinning the rattle above his head and yelling at the top of his voice, 'Get back! Run! Run! They'll shoot!'

He hardly noticed Joseph and Afra close beside him, banging the saucepan lids together and pounding on the drum. He was aware only of the leopard, which had turned in one easy, fluid movement and had bounded into the cover of the undergrowth where he had disappeared, his camouflage of spots making him instantly invisible.

Tom turned at once, and saw that the Hovens had gone. He could hear their feet stumbling on the loose stones as they fled back up the hillside towards their house. An enormous sense of triumph filled him. He ripped off his stocking mask and flung it in the air.

He was just about to shout, 'We did it! We

saved him!' when Joseph shook his arm and put his finger to his lips, though his eyes were sparkling with delight.

'Perhaps they'll hear us and realize that we're only kids,' he whispered. 'Wait until they've gone far away.'

Tom nodded, listening to the fading sounds of the Hovens' retreat. Afra, restraining herself with difficulty from whooping aloud, expressed her feelings by standing on her hands. Joseph, beside her, began leaping up and down, executing a silent victory dance, his feet pounding rhythmically on the hard earth, his arms happily flailing the air. Tom joined in, and a moment later all three, suppressing their giggles, fell exhausted to the ground.

'Did you see their faces?' whispered Tom. 'I didn't. I was too busy watching the leopard.'

'I saw them,' said Joseph. 'That man, Mr Hoven, he looked very very angry. He turned his gun and pointed it in our direction. I thought he was going to shoot us. Then the boy pulled his arm so that the gun pointed away from us.'

'Pieter? Pieter did that?' said Tom.

'Mr Hoven, he hit Pieter on the side of the head, then he began to run away. Pieter went after him.'

'Wow!' said Tom. 'You mean Mr Hoven was going to shoot us and Pieter stopped him?'

'I don't think he was going to shoot us really.' Joseph shook his head. 'Maybe for one second, perhaps, but not even that bully man would be so crazy to . . .'

'Oh, I don't know about that,' said Afra. 'He was planning on shooting the leopard, after all. And that means big trouble if he's found out. It would have been a crazy thing to do. And for a guy like that, a bunch of kids wouldn't count.'

A loud hoot interrupted her and she turned to see Kiksy bounding across the ground towards her. She bent down and lifted the bushbaby into her arms.

'Where did you go, Kiksy?' she said. 'You'd better stay close to me now. Maybe that leopard didn't go so far away.'

Tom shivered and looked round uneasily. He had been feeling entirely safe, but suddenly he wasn't so sure.

'You mean he might be lying in wait somewhere? He might still go for us?' he said.

'No,' said Joseph. 'I don't think he will attack us, at least while we're together. But we're in danger if we're alone.'

'I just couldn't believe how fast he disappeared,' said Tom. 'I mean, one minute he was there, the next it was just bushes. You couldn't tell his spots for leaves.'

Joseph nodded. He looked serious again.

'But we've only saved him for now. Tonight, when he's hungry, he'll hunt again. He's already started to take the pets around the houses here.

144

They're easy prey for him. I think he'll try again. I don't think we've driven him far enough away.'

Tom, thinking of Tiger, was about to answer when he heard, from the hillside behind them, a faint voice carrying down on the wind. It was Debbie's.

'Tom!' she was calling. 'Where are you? *Tom!*'

Tom's heart sank.

'Oh no! That's Mum,' he said. 'They're back and they've found out I've gone. I've got to go.'

He set off up the path with the others close behind him. Joseph, reckoning that the Hovens were well out of earshot by now, was giving little whoops of victory, dancing as he trotted up the path. Afra was echoing him, laughing as Kiksy tickled her ear. But Tom wasn't feeling triumphant any longer. He had another battle to fight now, the battle with Mum and Dad.

'See you,' he said breathlessly to the others, when he came to the place where he had to dive down under the bushes to reach the gap in his fence. 'I'll leave you a message as soon as I can.'

He hesitated when he reached the chain link and scanned the garden, unwilling to go through it if anyone was watching in case he gave it away. No one was in sight.

Screwing his courage up, he squeezed through it and walked purposefully up the garden, across the verandah and into the sitting room.

In the front hall beyond, he could hear his mother speaking on the telephone.

'What?' she was saying. 'What do you mean, Lise? He *didn't* come round yesterday to borrow Pieter's atlas?'

Then his father, who had been pacing up and down the narrow front hall beside her, saw Tom and snatched the receiver out of Debbie's hands.

'It's all right,' he said curtly. 'Tom's just turned up. Sorry to have troubled you.'

He put the receiver down and both parents turned furiously on Tom.

'Where on *earth* . . .?' began Debbie.

'What the *devil* . . .?' said Simon.

'OK, I'm sorry. I'm really, really sorry,' said Tom hastily. 'Listen, I'm going to tell you everything. It's OK. Everything's really OK.'

'Well, I've heard it all now. You think everything's OK, do you?' Simon's voice was heavy with sarcasm. 'You set all this up, didn't you? Left a note on your door, left your radio on, pretended you were doing your homework, when all the time . . .'

'Oh Tom, how could you?' wailed Debbie, dabbing her eyes. 'I've been so worried about you. We've been searching for you everywhere for hours and hours. Look at your face! And why are you wearing that filthy old sweater? It's much too hot today. What have you been *doing*?'

'Look,' said Tom desperately. 'It's just that I've

made some new friends. They're really great and I like them.'

'What friends?' Debbie looked suspicious. 'Where do they come from? Have you met their families? Who . . .'

'Mum,' said Tom irritably, 'they're *friends*. Just friends, all right?'

'It's those people next door, I suppose.' Debbie was frowning now.

'What people next door?' said Simon.

'Yes, they are the people next door,' said Tom defiantly, 'and they're called Afra and Joseph and they're great, and Afra's got a bushbaby called Kiksy, and if you really want to know, it was her atlas I borrowed because she's in my year at school, and I never went near Pieter Hoven and I'm never going to because he's a loudmouth and a bully and . . .'

Suddenly, he remembered how Pieter had knocked his dad's gun off its aim and he stopped.

Simon's mouth was twitching.

'That's all very well, Tom,' he said, in a much milder voice. 'But if you wanted to go and play next door, why didn't you tell us where you were going? It was very inconsiderate.'

'Because Mum said I wasn't to,' said Tom, sensing that Simon was an ally now and transferring his gaze to him. 'That dentist woman, Mrs Whassername, told Mum they were a bunch of weirdos, but they're not. Afra's mum's dead, but her dad's an archaeologist. He's got loads of broken pottery in his study.'

He paused and looked across at Debbie. She was wavering, he could see that.

'You didn't like Scott at first,' he said accusingly.

Debbie, finding both Simon's and Tom's eyes fixed reproachfully on her, opened her mouth, but not knowing what to say, shut it again.

I've got to tell them about the leopard, thought Tom. I promised myself I would.

'Listen,' he said, gearing himself up for another storm. 'There's something else I've got to tell you.'

The chimes on the wall above his head burst into life as someone rang the front doorbell.

'That can't be the Hovens already, can it?' whispered Debbie, aghast, running her hands over her hair. 'The sitting room's still a total tip! Tom, quick, get in there and plump the cushions up!'

But Tom was halfway up the stairs. He couldn't face the Hovens yet. He needed time to calm down, to hide his stocking mask, which was still in his pocket, and change his sweater in case they recognized it.

He bolted into his room, stuffed the mask behind his pillow, tore off his sweater and dropped it in the corner. Then he pulled on a fresh T-shirt with the Aston Villa logo on it.

He looked round his room. He wouldn't bother

to tidy up. There was no way he was going to let Pieter Hoven come up here.

He was on his way out again when he caught sight of his face in the mirror opposite the window. Traces of mud from the mask still clung to it. He went to the bathroom and washed it, towelled it dry, then, with a sinking heart, walked down the stairs.

He heard voices from the sitting room and opened the door. A strange man was standing by the verandah doors, talking to his parents. He was a tall, good-looking African, wearing a neat khaki uniform with the letters KWS emblazoned on the shoulder flash.

And beside him, grinning broadly, were Afra and Joseph.

16

UNCLE TITUS

'Ah, here's Tom,' said Simon. 'Tom, come and say hello to Mr Musau. He's from the Kenya Wildlife Service.'

'It's Uncle Titus,' mouthed Afra, from behind Simon's back.

Titus Musau put out his hand.

'So this is Tom!' he said genially. 'Afra and Joseph have told me many things about you.'

Behind his back, Afra and Joseph looked at each other and turned apologetically to Tom.

'We told him not to say anything,' Afra hissed. 'He forgot.'

'It's OK,' Tom whispered back. 'I told Mum and Dad we were friends. I told them I was going to see you whenever I liked and I don't care what they say. Dad's OK. It's Mum who makes the fuss.'

But Afra and Joseph's attention had snapped back to Uncle Titus, who was still talking to Simon and Debbie.

'. . . probably no danger to people,' he was saying. 'Leopards have been known to attack human beings but only on rare occasions. The problem we have is that this leopard has become accustomed to easy prey, such as domestic pets. Dogs and cats are very easy for him to catch.'

'Beatrice's poor little dog!' gasped Debbie. 'How terrible!'

'What's your strategy?' said Simon. 'How do you tackle this kind of thing? I mean we can't just have a dangerous wild animal on the loose in an urban area like this.'

'Our final option is extermination,' said Uncle Titus, looking down across the lawn towards the forest edge beyond. 'We have marksmen who are very experienced in this kind of thing.'

'*No!*' A dark tide was welling up in Afra's brown cheeks. 'Uncle Titus, you said you wouldn't shoot him! You can't shoot him. Leopards were here before people. He has a right to live here. He's wild and free and beautiful and he can't be allowed to die!'

'You mean you've seen it?' said Debbie, aghast. 'Not actually near a house or anything, was it?'

'Yes. We've all seen him,' said Afra. 'I wasn't as close as Tom, though.'

'Tom? You saw a leopard close to our house and you didn't tell us?' Debbie was flushed with indignation.

'I was going to,' said Tom. 'I wanted to, but I knew you'd only panic and get him shot.'

'It was extremely irresponsible of you,' said Simon, looking annoyed. 'You might have thought of Tiger. And what would have happened if Bella had wandered off on her own?'

'Bella! A leopard! Oh my God!'

Debbie snatched Bella up off one of the basket-work chairs where she'd been quietly absorbed in an incomprehensible muttered conversation with her doll. Bella struggled in her arms and reluctantly Debbie put her down again.

'Please,' said Afra, looking at Debbie, 'don't be mad with Tom. It was my fault. I made him promise not to tell, so we could think how to save the leopard ourselves. And Tom was so brave. Why, when Mr Hoven was about to shoot the leopard, Tom ran right out and scared him off.'

Simon had squatted down to pick up Bella's doll, which had fallen to the ground, but he straightened up at once.

'Rudi Hoven?' he said. 'What's he got to do with this?'

'I believe that this man, Mr Hoven, has attempted to take the law into his own hands and has tried to hunt the leopard using his shotgun,' said Uncle Titus with heavy disapproval.

A smile began to blossom on Simon's face.

'That's illegal, isn't it?'

'It is a serious breach of the law, Mr Wilkinson.'

'Are you going to get the police to charge him?' Simon half turned away, in an unsuccessful attempt to hide his eagerness.

'Unfortunately that is impossible as there were no witnesses to the offence,' said Uncle Titus.

'What do you mean, Uncle Titus? We were witnesses. We saw him,' Afra burst out.

'Children are not admissable as witnesses in a court of law,' said Uncle Titus.

Afra stared up at him with stormy eyes.

'Anyway,' she said, 'I don't see why you should care if Mr Hoven tried to shoot the leopard or not, since you're going to shoot him yourself.'

Uncle Titus frowned.

'Afra, I didn't say we're going to shoot the leopard,' he began.

'Yes, you did. You said . . .'

'That bushbaby's brains have got tangled up with your brains, Afra. I said we have to exterminate the leopard only as a last resort. But first we try something else. Just like you did. We will attempt to frighten him, to make him leave this area.'

'Like they did?' said Simon, puzzled. 'What did they do?'

'Tom was very brave.' Joseph, who had been hanging back shyly, smiled at Simon. 'He ran out when Mr Hoven came with his gun and scared the leopard away with his football rattle.'

'You went after a leopard armed only with Dad's old football rattle?' said Simon incredulously.

'We had some saucepan lids and Joseph's drum too,' said Afra.

'And it worked,' said Tom. 'The leopard ran away.'

'I'll bet,' grinned Simon. 'I'll bet Rudi Hoven ran away too. One look at you and he'd have bolted up the nearest tree.'

'Oh, I don't think he recognized us,' Tom said. 'We were disguised.'

'What with?' Simon was chuckling now. 'False beards? Face paints? Hallowe'en masks?'

'Not exactly.' Tom shot a nervous glance at Debbie. 'I was going to tell you before, honestly, Mum. We . . . I . . . Well, I nicked a couple of pairs of tights out of your drawer and we put them over our heads like bank robbers.'

Simon threw his head back and roared with laughter. Debbie frowned.

'You should have asked,' she said. 'I don't like you messing about with my stuff.'

Simon wiped his eyes.

'Oh come on, Debs,' he said. 'Where's your sense of humour? I just wish I'd seen it, that's all. Especially the expression on Rudi Hoven's face. Scared off by a bunch of kids with football rattles and tights over their faces!'

Afra thought of something and turned to Uncle Titus.

'Maybe we scared him off, enough,' she said. 'Maybe he's gone anyway.'

Uncle Titus nodded.

'It's possible,' he said, 'but I don't think so. We have to make sure.'

'What do you use for this sort of thing?' said Simon, interested. 'Sirens?'

'No,' said Uncle Titus. 'We have found that the most effective method is the use of thunderflashes.'

'Thunderflashes?' Simon was in a rollicking good mood now. He slapped his thigh. 'Mate of mine was in the army,' he said. 'One night they all got a bit merry and he chucked a thunderflash down inside a piano. Said he'd never heard anything like it. Every chord known to the human ear and a bang you could have heard halfway to the moon. Wrecked the piano, of course.'

Uncle Titus looked disapproving.

'It's important to use very stringent safety measures,' he said. 'There is some risk of injury to personnel.'

'I know, I know,' said Simon hastily. 'Like I said, they were tanked up.'

In the hall, the clock chimed.

'Is that the time?' said Debbie. 'The Hovens'll be here any minute. What are we going to do?'

'We're going to enjoy ourselves, that's what,' said Simon, rubbing his hands. 'I'll get the drinks ready.'

'Look at all this mess in here,' said Debbie, stepping back from the verandah into the sitting room. Excuse me, Mr Musau. I must just tidy up a bit.'

She began picking up empty mugs and putting them down on a tray.

'Can I help you, Mrs Wilkinson?' said Afra.

'May I carry that tray for you?' said Joseph, taking it out of her hands.

Debbie looked at them helplessly.

'It has to go in the kitchen,' she said. 'You don't know where that is.'

'Yes, we do,' said Afra. 'We used to be friends with Susie, who lived here before you came.'

'Oh! Susie Chalmers!' said Debbie, her face clearing. 'You knew the Chalmers then, did you?'

'Sure. We were really good friends,' said Afra.

Debbie was looking after Joseph, who was taking the tray out of the room.

'Just put it down on the kitchen table,' she said, following him.

'It's all right, you don't have to do all this stuff,' said Tom. 'I told her about you. It's OK.'

Afra looked crossly at him.

'You think I'm just greasing up to her, don't you?' she said. 'You weren't brought up by Sarah. She has these far-out ideas on how to be a good guest and helpful and stuff like that. We've been trained. Like performing seals.'

She began to plump up the cushions on the sofa. Debbie came back into the room.

'Who taught you to do that, dear?' she said.

Afra stiffened. Tom held his breath.

'Sarah, Joseph's mom,' she said. 'She brought me up. My mother was Ethiopian. She's dead.'

'Oh, how . . . I didn't mean . . .' said Debbie, flustered. She smiled at Afra. 'Tom tells me you've become great friends. That's lovely. I hope you'll come round and play with him sometimes.'

Afra looked sideways at Joseph.

'And – it's Joseph, isn't it? – can come too, of course,' said Debbie hastily.

Uncle Titus stepped forward.

'I'm glad you approve of these young rascals,' he said. 'If they give you any trouble, just get in touch with the KWS. We'll send our men down with some thunderflashes to scare them off.'

Debbie laughed.

'Oh, I'm sure that won't be necessary,' she said. 'They seem like very nice children. Very polite.'

Simon came back into the room with a tray of bottles and glasses in his hands.

'What'll you have, Mr Musau?' he said.

Uncle Titus shook his head.

'Thanks, but I have to go now. My team is visiting all the houses in the area to warn them that there will be some very loud bangs shortly. I have to check on their progress.'

'Another time, perhaps,' said Simon, slapping him on the back.

'Simon, the Hovens are here,' said Debbie,

running into the room. 'I saw them from the kitchen window.'

'On second thoughts,' said Uncle Titus, 'perhaps I will stay for a few minutes longer. I would like to see this man who thinks he has the right to shoot a leopard in defiance of the law!'

17

THUNDERFLASHES
IN THE FOREST

Simon went out into the hall and opened the front door.

'Mr Hoven! Come in!' the others heard him say. 'And you're Mrs Hoven? And this must be Pieter, I suppose.'

There was a short pause.

'You've done well for yourself, I must say,' Mr Hoven said in a jeering voice, obviously looking round the hall. 'A lot more palatial than what you were used to back in England, eh?'

'Oh, we didn't do so badly at home,' said Simon cheerfully. 'We've got a very nice semi in a quiet road. Going up in value all the time.'

There was a heavy silence.

'Why doesn't he bring them in here?' said Debbie, going to the sitting room door.

Tom, Afra and Joseph looked nervously at each other. They heard Debbie say, 'Hello, Lise. So glad you could make it. And you must be Pieter.'

'Stop staring like that, Pieter,' came Mr Hoven's curt voice. 'Shake hands.'

'Come into the sitting room,' said Debbie.

'Yes.' Simon could hardly control the eagerness

in his voice. 'There's someone here I'd like you to meet.'

He stood back as Debbie led the three Hovens into the sitting room. Pieter came in last. Unnoticed by the adults, he stuck his tongue out at Tom and rolled his eyes derisively.

Tom and Afra both made faces back at him, noticed each other doing it and giggled.

'Let me introduce you to Joseph,' said Tom, putting on Debbie's hostess voice. 'I don't think you've met.'

'No, but I've seen you somewhere before,' said Joseph. He put his head on one side as if he was trying to remember, and stared unsmilingly at Pieter. 'I wonder where that was?' The sneer dropped from Pieter's face. He looked a little anxious.

Simon had darted forward.

'I don't suppose you know Mr Musau,' he said to the Hovens. 'He's from the Kenya Wildlife Service.'

Uncle Titus put his hand out. Mr Hoven didn't shake it. His face had become expressionless.

'Mr Musau's just been telling us the most extra-ordinary things,' Simon went on, his eyes fixed on Mr Hoven's face.

'Yes. I have been informing Mr Wilkinson of the leopard that has been roaming in the strip of forest behind these properties,' said Uncle Titus. 'Do you have any knowledge of it?'

'A leopard?' Mr Hoven licked his lips. 'No, no. Why would I know anything about a leopard?'

'Amazing, isn't it?' Simon was still staring unblinkingly at Mr Hoven. 'Apparently, some nutter went after it with a gun.'

Mr Hoven's heavy red face turned a little pale.

'It was a very foolish thing to do,' said Uncle Titus gravely, tucking his thumbs into his highly polished leather belt. 'Are you aware, Mr Hoven, of the penalties for the illegal shooting of a protected animal?'

Tom could see that Pieter was scared. His eyes were darting between Uncle Titus and his father.

'Me? Why should I know about that sort of thing?' Mr Hoven blustered. 'Hunting's not in my line at all.'

'Yes it is, dear,' said Lise Hoven innocently. 'You and Mr De Wit used to go out after antelope all the time in . . .'

Her voice died away as she read the fury in her husband's narrowed eyes.

'Who'd like a drink?' said Debbie brightly. 'Simon, aren't you going to do the honours?'

'Thank you, but not for me,' said Uncle Titus. 'I must go. Remember, don't be afraid when you hear the thunderflashes.'

'They're going to scare the leopard away,' said Afra to Pieter, who didn't look at her.

Uncle Titus was at the sitting room door now. He turned and said, 'If you should ever discover who it was who tried to shoot the leopard, Mr Hoven, you will inform me, please.'

'Yes, of course, I . . .' stammered Mr Hoven.

'Apparently,' said Simon, grinning broadly, 'the guy was scared off by three kids waving football rattles and banging saucepan lids. Hilarious, isn't it?'

Mr Hoven tried to laugh, and failed.

'He'd be a laughing stock if it ever got out,' Simon went on, following Uncle Titus out of the room. His voice floated back from the hall. 'Yes, and thank you very much too, Mr Musau. Oh sure. We'll let you know if we find out who it was. Good luck tonight.'

'You still haven't had a drink!' said Debbie. 'Lise, what'll it be?'

'Oh, just a bitter lemon, if you've got any,' said Mrs Hoven faintly.

'And you'll have a whisky, Mr Hoven, won't you?' said Simon, coming back into the room.

'Rudi,' said Mr Hoven, drawing his lips back from his teeth in an unpractised effort to smile. 'Call me Rudi.'

'Let's go up to my room,' said Tom suddenly, unable to hold in for a second longer the laughter that was threatening to overwhelm him.

He dashed to the door. Afra and Joseph followed him.

'Go on up with them, Pieter,' said Debbie kindly, giving Pieter a little push. 'Don't be shy.'

Tom made it into his room, flung himself down on his bed and muffled his howls of laughter in his pillow. Afra and Joseph fell on top of him.

'Did you see his face when your dad said that bit about the saucepan lids?' gasped Afra.

' "Are you aware of the penalties for shooting a leopard?" ' panted Joseph, imitating Uncle Titus.

' "Call me Rudi"!' wailed Tom, and he collapsed on to his pillow again.

He became aware, a moment later, that Afra and Joseph had stopped laughing. He lifted his head and looked round. Pieter was standing at the bedroom door.

For a moment no one said anything, then Pieter turned back towards the head of the stairs.

'No, it's OK, you can come in,' said Tom.

Pieter advanced slowly into the room.

'It's all right for you,' he said. 'You don't have to live with him.'

He flopped down onto the bed and burst into tears.

The others looked at each other over his head. Joseph was the first to move. He sat down beside him and gently shook his arm.

'Pieter,' he said. 'We weren't laughing at you.'

Pieter wiped his nose savagely across his sleeve. He pointed to Tom's sweater, lying in the corner of the room.

'It was you down there, wasn't it?' he said. 'You

were wearing that sweater. I knew it was you all the time. You'll tell them all at school, I suppose.'

'I won't,' said Afra.

'*He* will.' Pieter looked at Tom. 'I suppose I would if I was him.'

'I won't if you get off my back and stop getting at me,' said Tom.

'I was only joking anyway,' said Pieter. 'Only teasing.'

Tom picked up his stocking mask, which had worked its way out from under his pillow, and started weaving it between his fingers.

'It didn't feel like it was only teasing.'

Pieter dropped his eyes.

'It's all right for you,' he said again. 'People like you. You've only been here five minutes and you've got friends already.'

'What do you mean?' Tom was indignant. 'You've got masses of friends. They hang around with you all the time.'

'They're not friends,' said Pieter contemptuously. 'They're scared of me.'

'Oh wow, that's horrible,' said Afra. 'I guess we could be friends with you, maybe.'

Joseph grinned.

'If anybody is my friend, I am their friend,' he said, and he slapped his hand down onto Pieter's open palm and shook it.

Pieter looked up at Tom.

'Yeah, I suppose so,' said Tom, 'but only if you lay off me.'

'Oh I will,' said Pieter. 'I won't tease you any more. Honestly.'

'Or anyone else, for that matter,' said Afra, frowning at him.

Tom grinned at him.

'We all owe you one, anyway,' he said. 'You knocked your dad's gun off its aim.'

Pieter chuckled. His face changed and he looked much nicer.

'You should have seen yourselves prancing round with those stocking things over your heads,' he said. 'I've never seen anything like it.'

'Do you want a go?' said Tom, handing him his mask.

Pieter put it on, jumped up and started bounding round the room, shouting, 'This is a stick-up! Hand over the cash!'

Suddenly he stopped, ripped off the mask and pointed to the window.

'What on earth's that?' he said.

The others turned. Kiksy was sitting on the windowsill, one little hand pressed against the glass, his huge eyes fixed longingly on Afra.

'Kiksy!' said Afra, opening the window.

The bushbaby ran up to her shoulder and flung a long hairy arm round her neck.

'Oh, he's beautiful,' breathed Pieter. 'Can I touch him?'

'Sure,' said Afra. 'Gently, though.'

'Tom!' Debbie's voice came floating up the stairs. 'The Hovens have to go now. Come and say goodbye.'

Pieter's face fell.

'I've got to go,' he said, 'and Dad'll be in a filthy temper.'

'Tell him you're staying on here for a bit,' said Afra.

'Are you kidding?' Pieter said. 'He'd kill me.'

Tom clapped him on the shoulder.

'We'll see you on Monday, anyway. And maybe they'll let you come over again tomorrow.'

Pieter smiled wanly.

'You don't know my dad,' he said.

Tom, Afra and Joseph wandered out into the garden. It was evening now. The brilliance of the African day was fading fast into the velvet darkness of the African night.

'When'll they do it?' said Tom. 'The thunder-flashes, I mean.'

'They'll do it when they find him, I think,' said Joseph. 'They're looking for him now.'

Afra shivered.

'Poor leopard. On his own. He'll be so frightened.'

'He's got to learn, though, hasn't he?' said Tom. 'He can't go on hanging round people and eating their pets. He's got to be a proper wild leopard and be independent and stick to eating baby antelopes and hares and stuff.'

'I know,' said Afra, 'but it must be kind of lonesome out there.'

'Afra,' said Joseph. 'You're too soft. Leopards aren't people. They have their own nature. They like to live on their own. You're not like him and he's not like you. Especially when you have that bushbaby on your shoulder. He would eat him first thing.'

'It's so boring when you're right all the time,' said Afra.

'I'm right, I'm right, I'm right all the time,' said Joseph, banging himself on the chest and pirouetting round. 'Hey, Tom, is that your sister?'

The others turned. Bella was running towards them across the grass. She grabbed Tom's leg and looked shyly up at Afra and Joseph. Joseph squatted down and started making funny faces at her. Afra looked at her critically.

'I don't know much about little kids,' she said.

Joseph made a mouse shape with his hand and ran it across the grass towards Bella. She squealed with laughter and tightened her grip on Tom's knee.

'She's cute,' said Afra.

'She's a pain,' said Tom. 'You can have her.'

Afra was shocked.

'You can't say that about your own sister,' she said. 'I'd give anything to have one.'

'You wouldn't,' said Tom. 'You don't know what it's like. I'd rather have a bushbaby any time.'

'You wouldn't.'

'I would.'

'You wouldn't. You don't know what you're talking about.'

'OK,' said Tom, discovering that he was rather enjoying the clutch of Bella's warm little arms round his knee, and was even proud of the attention she was getting. 'Maybe I wouldn't.'

'Bella!' Debbie called from the verandah steps. 'Come to Mummy. It's bathtime.'

Obediently, Bella trotted away.

The last streaks of orange light on the horizon were fading to purple. The heavy scent of waxy white flowers on the frangipani tree near the house wafted across the garden, and underneath it, in the grass, unseen crickets buzzed furiously. Kiksy, who had been resting quietly on Afra's shoulder, took off in a long smooth leap and returned a moment later with a big insect in his hand. He crunched it happily, swivelling his head as his eyes and ears probed the darkness.

A violent bang suddenly split the air and a brilliant flash lit up their three faces.

'There it is. They've found the leopard,' said Joseph.

The thunderflash had caused mayhem in the forest. Birds were shrieking out alarm calls. Far away, a troop of monkeys chattered and screamed with fear, and on all sides dogs were barking, egging each other on, filling the night with a cacophony of sound. Men's voices, too, came floating up from the forest below. They were shouting excitedly.

'We could have gone down there and helped them,' said Joseph regretfully.

'I wouldn't want to,' said Afra. 'I don't want to see him running away, all scared and humiliated.'

Another bang came from further down the valley.

'They're flushing him out,' Joseph said, measuring the distance in his mind. 'They'll frighten him far away from where the people live.'

Tom imagined the leopard, racing through the undergrowth, fleeing from the noise and light, his muscles bunching and stretching, his eyes piercing the dark. What was it that had driven him out of his old home in the first place? Would he dare go back there? Or would he try to find somewhere new to live and hunt?

He looked up. A few early stars were out, piercing the black sky with pinpricks of light, but he could still make out the line of the Ngong hills in the distance, their black shape fading almost as he watched into the indigo sky.

Perhaps, he thought, the leopard would make for the hills, creeping stealthily along trails he'd known before, that only leopards knew. Perhaps he'd find a good place, with plenty of game, and trees to hide in, and a nice stream to drink from. He'd find it tough at first, getting used to a new home, and maybe he'd have to fight it out with other leopards before they'd let him stay. But he might settle down in time.

'Good luck, mate,' he said. 'I hope you make it out there.'